MW01601384

The

Good Wife

B.M. Roberts

Raven House Press

The Good Wife

© 2025 B.M. Roberts

Acknowledgments

For information, contact:

www.bmrobertsauthor.com

ISBN [979-8-3493-7728-0]

Printed in the United States of America

Raven House Press

For the wives and the mothers —

the ones who hold it all together with trembling hands and
teeth clenched in a smile.

For those who bury their pain beneath clean countertops and
soft apologies,

who are expected to forgive everything,

endure anything, and

disappear gracefully.

This is for you.

You were never just a wife.

Never only a mother.

You were the whole foundation —   and

the spark that could burn it all down.

Table of Contents

Prologue

Room 604
Mason Hill Hotel and Conference Center

The killer watched the hallway for exactly thirty-six minutes before she arrived.

The elevator chimed softly — discreet, forgettable — and then the doors opened. She stepped out in a black coat that fell just below the knee, a wig cut in a sharp, severe line framing her face. Green contact lenses. No jewelry. Heels muted by the carpet. She walked like someone who didn't want to be followed but knew how to be seen. The posture of control, not seduction. Of detachment.

The killer didn't move from his post near the corner suite. He didn't need to.
He had already memorized the room number. Already traced the path she'd take. He just wanted to watch her face, to see if she hesitated. She didn't.
Delia. That was the name she used in her secret life. Not her real one — he knew that. He'd known it for months, had run her name against every encrypted record he still had access

to, even the ones he wasn't supposed to. But "Delia" was the name she went by in this circle. A mask with perfect seams. And tonight, it was the only one that mattered.

The man who opened the door was disgusting. Broad hands. Greedy eyes. Thin lips stretched too wide in greeting. He ushered her in with the breathless entitlement of someone who had paid, and therefore believed he owned the moment. Owned her.

David Holbrook.

That was the name used for the booking.

He hadn't known who the man really was — not at first. That came later, after he started digging. The hotel, the burner line, the bank transfer that stank of corporate laundering. The details led to a name, and that name led to an address. The address to a woman. A wife.

That's when the rage crystallized.

Because that woman — the oblivious, well-groomed wife on the charity circuit — wasn't some stranger. She was family. Not by choice, but by blood. And the man in Room 604 wasn't just a predator. He was something much closer.

The kind of close that demanded consequences.

The file had been building for years. Whisper networks. Redacted reports. Girls who vanished from booking sites without explanation. One hospital record never followed up on. One girl who said no, and woke up in a stairwell with

6

broken ribs and no memory of how she got there. And still he walked free, his name never making it into headlines. Too connected. Too careful.

Until now.

The killer shifted slightly, the corner of his coat brushing the doorframe.

Not long now.

He waited thirteen more minutes.

Long enough to confirm what he already suspected — Delia was stalling. That's what she always did when she sensed something was off. The pause between a greeting and a transaction. The verbal dance. The negotiations. Her way of regaining the upper hand.

She would be cool, firm, detached. She never let them touch her before it was time. She liked to pace the room, to make them wait. And he knew that David — glutton that he was — wouldn't like that. Would start pressing. Wouldn't be able to help himself.

He didn't flinch at the thought. He didn't let himself think about her in there, not exactly. This wasn't about her.

She was nothing.

She'd made her choices. Sold herself like a product. Traded decency for cash, attention, power. He didn't care what happened to her. Didn't care what any of these girls endured.

They were whores, every one of them. They invited this.

Filth feeding on filth, and he hated the whole filthy circuit. The way they smiled and strutted and pretended they weren't asking for it. The way they pretended to be victims when things turned ugly. He didn't care what these clients did to whores. That was their world, not his.

But David?

David was family.

And family had boundaries. Family had rules. David had violated both.

He could degrade strangers — that was expected, even tolerated — but dragging someone from his own bloodline into this sewer? That was grotesque. That was unforgivable.

David had dragged someone into it who mattered. Someone who shared his blood.

That made it personal.

David cheating on someone in the family — that wasn't a lapse in judgment. That was rot. That was a betrayal so base, so grotesque, it demanded punishment. Abolishment.

A paper trail was traced back two months earlier. A string of calls from the same burner number. Obsessive patterns.

Demands for Delia. Only her. The agency had flagged him as a repeat, a high-tipper with boundary issues. One handler called him a "collector." The kind of man who wanted ownership.

And still, he'd gotten through.

And now she was inside Room 604 with a man who once pinned a girl to a marble bathroom counter and said she should be grateful he didn't leave marks. Who paid extra for silence. Who donated to anti-trafficking charities with the same hands he used to choke out consent.

The man who, until last week, the killer had known only as a name on a sheet.
A name that turned out to be carved into his own family tree.

He didn't remember opening the supply closet, didn't feel the weight of the server's uniform as he pulled it on. His body moved without thought.

Now there was just the hallway again. The cart. The tray. The silver dome covering an invisible meal no one ordered.

She left the room with her head high and her voice low — sharp, clipped words whispered into the burner phone held tight against her cheek. The door clicked shut behind her, and for a moment, the hallway swallowed her whole. She didn't look back. Her exit was deliberate, rehearsed. She'd done this before.

She was meant to be in the room too, but he wanted this done. And David was his real focus. He waited. Let a full thirty seconds bleed out before stepping forward.

He slid the keycard in and waited for the green light, and then walked into the room without knocking.

The room was dim, just as he'd hoped. The heavy blackout curtains were already drawn, leaving the place in a syrupy twilight that muddled all sharp lines. He wore the hotel uniform he'd swiped from the service closet — collared shirt, name tag, cap pulled low — and kept his shoulders slouched to further blur the silhouette. A tray in his hands, white cloth folded neatly over his fingers. Just another anonymous worker doing his rounds.

David was reclined on the corner of the bed, undressed from the waist up, shoes off, half a drink already in hand. A crystal glass, probably hotel-stocked bourbon. The man looked relaxed — too relaxed. That smug ease of someone who believed himself untouchable.

And for most of his life, he had been.

Predators like David didn't usually stumble. They climbed. Quietly, strategically. They made themselves indispensable in boardrooms and palatable at dinner parties. They wore loyalty like a badge and their wives like accessories, and when they strayed, they did so with the precision of men who'd studied the art of getting away with it.

The killer had known about the escorts. The hush money. The settlements wrapped in NDAs. He'd pieced it together over the last few weeks — one breadcrumb at a time. Each discovery sharpening the contours of the man now seated in front of him.

But the connection had come later. The moment that nearly derailed everything.

His name.

His real name.

Not David Holbrook, but a last name that was far more familiar.

The blood had drained from his face when the truth landed — this wasn't just another client. This wasn't a stranger. This was family. And not distant family, either. Someone who should have been unrecognizable only because it was unthinkable.

But now, as he stood in the doorway, watching David drink and stretch and smirk into the hotel dusk, he was glad for the shadows. Glad for the cap and the stoop in his posture and the half-turned face. Because David would've known him — instantly.

And that recognition would have ruined everything.

The door clicked shut behind him.

David didn't look up.
"Finally," he muttered, assuming it was her again. "Took you long enough."

The killer said nothing.

He crossed the room quietly, placing the tray on the low dresser by the wall-mounted TV. The cloth covering it slipped off with a controlled sweep. On the dresser stood a heavy crystal vase. The kind that was used as a decorative piece only. Now it would be repurposed.

He picked it up with one hand.

Behind him, David shifted. "You forgot the—"

He didn't get to finish.

The first blow came fast and flat to the base of his skull. A sharp, concussive crack. David jerked forward with a low grunt, still clutching the tumbler, his brain struggling to register what had just happened.

The second strike caught him at the temple.
The third — clean and brutal — landed squarely on the top of the head.

He collapsed off the side of the bed, hitting the carpet with a sickening thud, limbs twitching for a moment before going still. His drink rolled to a stop beneath the nightstand, leaving a trail of cheap scotch along the floor. The only sound now was the hum of the air conditioner and the faint click of a neon sign outside the window.

Blood pooled quickly beneath him, already soaking into the fibers. His body settled awkwardly, twisted at the waist, one arm curled uselessly over his stomach like he was trying to hold something in.

The vase went back on the tray. He turned it so the wiped handle faced forward again, cloth refolded. No fingerprints. No hesitation.

This was revenge.

And it had been delivered.

The killer waited.

Still, silent, tucked into the narrow shadow between the minibar and the heavy blackout drapes, where the lamplight didn't quite reach. The room was dim now, lit only by the faint bedside glow David had forgotten to switch off, and the low flicker from the muted television looping a hotel welcome screen. It cast a soft, eerie light across the bedspread — wrinkled now, and the carpet beneath, darkened with patches of blood that hadn't stopped spreading.

He hadn't fully expected her to come back, but then the hallway door cracked open, and she stepped back in.

She froze for a split second, silhouetted by the corridor light. The killer didn't move. She hadn't screamed. That was the most surprising part. Just stood there, one hand still gripping the edge of the doorframe, eyes locked on the dying man. Still gasping and choking on his own blood.

Then she moved.

Not toward him — but toward the dresser, where the envelope lay.

She picked it up without hesitation, like it had always belonged to her, like she had earned it. A glance over her shoulder, one breath — then she turned and walked out, letting the door fall shut behind her with a whisper of finality.

Only then did the killer exhale.

He waited in the dark for another minute, maybe two. Not because he was afraid. But because he wanted to be certain. That no one else would enter.

He stepped out into the center of the room, gaze settling once more on the body. Blood still pooled in slow, syrupy spirals across the carpet, soaking toward the corner. The man had twitched once more. Then gone still.

The killer knelt briefly beside the body, confirming what he already knew.

Gone.

He stood again, calm, precise, then walked to the table where the keycard lay. He didn't discard it. Just tucked it into his coat pocket along with a hotel matchbook.

He walked to the door and opened it just wide enough to peer into the hall. Still quiet. Still empty. He stepped out and closed the door behind him, not rushing, not hesitating, the soft click echoing like a final note.

No one noticed him as he left the Mason Hill Hotel and Conference Center.

No one ever did.

Chapter One

The Cup

Red. Too bold to be an accident. Too loud to be ignored. The color of danger, of appetite, of blood freshly spilled.

Claire Holloway had built her life to be bulletproof. But something had slipped through—a hairline fracture in the calm, a presence she hadn't invited.

The house was too quiet. Not peaceful—never that—but unnervingly hollow, like a stage after the curtain falls. No music. No movement. Just the low hum of the refrigerator and the distant tick of the thermostat shifting the air, as though the house were exhaling around her.

The cup sat in the center of the marble counter like it had always belonged. Ceramic, bone white, with a faint gold rim. The kind sold in curated kitchen sets meant to signal joy or simplicity or a woman who had her life together. Claire had bought them when she was pregnant with Sadie and when Mark was still coming home on time. They were supposed to mean something then. Stability, maybe. Harmony.

She used to love these cups, she'd used them for brunches or play dates with matching napkins and something sweet on the side.

She thought she'd packed it away with the rest, stored high in the cabinets above the pantry—safe, forgotten.

But this one—this particular cup—was wrong.

Not because of the cup itself. Because of the lipstick.

Not a soft coral or muted plum. Not the gentle, maternal tones that now lived in her makeup drawer. No, this was a deep, defiant crimson. The kind of shade you wore when you wanted to be noticed.

Desired. Dangerous.

It stained the rim in a sharp crescent, smudged just slightly on the inner curve, like someone had been mid-sip when interrupted. Red. A bold, demanding red Claire hadn't worn in over a year. Not since she buried Delia. Not since she watched David bleed out in a hotel room.

A shiver ran across her arms.

Outside, the sky was low and gunmetal gray, clouds pressing down like they knew too much. The hydrangeas outside the kitchen window hung low from the morning rain. The house creaked softly, wood adjusting to the pressure.

Claire turned, slowly, scanning the room.

Everything was exactly as it should be. The chairs tucked in. The granite wiped clean. The floor swept. Not a trace of anything out of place—except that one red stain, drying quietly on the lip of a cup meant for company.

"Mom! I can't find my Chromebook charger!"

Emma's voice carried from upstairs, shrill with tween urgency, slicing through the quiet like a thrown plate. Claire blinked, pulled from the trance of the cup, her eyes dragging reluctantly away.

"In the study!" she called back, louder than necessary. "Check the table in the corner!"

A beat of silence followed—then the heavy thud of preteen footsteps, a slammed drawer, and another shout of frustration. Claire didn't respond this time. Her attention had already returned to the cup. She took a step closer.

The lipstick was drying now. Slightly cracked at the edge, where moisture had pulled away from the ceramic. She leaned in, wrapped a dishtowel around her hand, and picked it up like evidence.

With an exhale, she rinsed the cup under warm water, watching the stain swirl down the drain in faint ribbons before tucking it into the dishwasher with shaking hands. Then, just as she closed the door, she reached for the strawberries on the counter. Routine. Rhythm. Keep moving. She began slicing, each cut crisp, deliberate.

Mark came down the stairs the way he always did - as though gravity owed him something, each step a dull punctuation against the silence she had so carefully cultivated. He rubbed his arms in a theatrical shiver as he crossed into the kitchen, already casting blame on the thermostat before speaking a single word. "It's freezing," he muttered, without looking at her, as if the chill in the air were a personal affront she'd engineered to make him uncomfortable.

Claire didn't answer at first. She was bent over Sadie's lunchbox, organizing crackers into the smallest compartment, not because it mattered, but because some part of her needed the illusion of control - of order, of precision, of normal.

It's seventy-two," she finally replied, not looking at him. "It always is."

He ignored her tone and dropped into the chair at the end of the island, already scrolling on his phone.

She slid a plate across to him. "Avocado toast. I added lemon."

Mark glanced up, briefly. "Thanks."

She moved to the Nespresso machine and prepared his coffee — dark roast, no foam, no sugar. She could do it in her sleep. Sometimes she suspected she had.

He took it without a word and sipped absently, scrolling through something that didn't deserve his attention.

And that was Mark now, after 12 years of marriage, bored and distant, but still a necessary fixture in their family, adored by their daughters, and Claire had long ago resolved to be the best wife she could possibly be.

She had loved him before things grew stale - really loved him, the kind of love that made her stomach tighten when his name lit up her phone, the kind that had made her believe in clean slates and second lives. In the beginning, Mark had been charming in that distracted, golden-boy way, all bright ideas and easy confidence, the kind of man who made waiters laugh and women lean forward at dinner parties. But over time, that light dimmed, or maybe it just shifted - became colder, less generous. Now their marriage felt like a sequence of habits performed with mutual precision: shared calendars, aligned dinner plans, perfectly timed silence. Still, every now and then, his words would twist a little too sharp, his compliments coated in control, and Claire would glimpse something deeper - something selfish and shining behind his eyes, like he still believed the world owed him more than it had given. And when she saw that flicker, she reminded herself: Be better. Be good. Keep him happy. You don't get to fall apart.

The sound of hurried footsteps on the stairs came first - two distinct rhythms, one heavier and pounding like thunder, the other quick and light, a scamper of small determination - and a moment later, Claire heard the slam of the upstairs bathroom door and the distinct clatter of something plastic bouncing down the final three steps.

Sadie arrived first, wrapped in fleece pants and a unicorn hoodie, her curls still damp and clinging to her forehead in wisps that smelled faintly of lavender de-tangler and sleep.

She burst into the kitchen in a gust of energy and chaos, wearing one pink sneaker and holding a half-colored school worksheet, the bunny she carried with her everywhere dangling limply from the crook of her arm.

"Mommy! I can't find my other shoe!" she wailed, as if the world might tilt off its axis if her second foot went unshod for even a moment longer.

Claire crouched automatically, her hands already in motion, brushing Sadie's hair back from her forehead, pressing a soft kiss to her temple, feeling the warm, living weight of her daughter's panic settle against her ribs like something she'd carried for years.

"It's probably under the couch," she said, her voice low, melodic, coaxing Sadie back from the ledge. "or the laundry basket. Check both, and come right back, baby."

"Okay!" Sadie shouted, already whirling around and disappearing down the hallway.

Emma followed next - older, taller, already in jeans and an obscure t shirt, her arms crossed, face set in the weary resignation of a girl who had learned to armor herself against the madness of mornings with silence and sarcasm.

"My green sweater shrunk mysteriously," Emma muttered, slinging her backpack over one shoulder as she slid onto the island stool, earbuds still loosely draped around her neck like jewelry she hadn't decided to wear yet.

Claire handed her a banana and half a granola bar wrapped in foil, not because Emma had asked for either, but because Claire knew - knew the way only mothers know the small, wordless languages of their children - that Emma wouldn't ask but still needed to be fed.

Mark stood suddenly, scraping his chair back with a noise louder than necessary, like he wanted the room to know he was still part of it, still a father, still somehow present even as his gaze remained tethered to the glowing rectangle in his hand.

"Let's go, I don't want to be late to work today," he said, already reaching for his keys.

Claire turned her head slowly, careful not to be too transparent by how she felt when he snapped at the girls.

"Okay everybody, have a great day!" she said, her voice light and airy, waving her daughters off with unconditional love.

Mark kissed her on the cheek, lightly, automatically, like pressing a stamp onto an envelope he wouldn't be reading. It was a gesture so hollow, so practiced, so entirely without weight that Claire felt her own body fail to register it as contact. It was nothing. A memory pretending to be a moment.

"Bye, Mommy!" Sadie sang, skipping past with her shoes finally on, her backpack bouncing with every step.

Emma followed, quieter, but she smiled because that was who she was: the child who smiled when she left, no matter how things felt inside. The front door closed.

The house was quiet again - unnaturally so, as though even the walls were waiting for her to make a sound, a decision, a mistake. Claire moved slowly across the kitchen, barefoot, the tile cool against her skin. Her hand hovered above the drawer near the fridge - the one that stuck slightly when pulled, the one no one else ever used.

She opened it, not all the way, just enough to slide her fingers to the back, where the space narrowed and dust gathered in corners no sponge ever reached.

The phone was there, tucked beneath a crumpled takeout menu and an old roll of Scotch tape, facedown, as if even it were ashamed of what it had once been. It was smaller than she remembered, and colder. Claire drew it out with two fingers, careful not to touch more of it than she had to, like it might burn her or brand her or speak her name aloud the moment it woke. She stared at it for a moment. Then, with a breath that felt rehearsed, she pressed the button.

The screen stayed dark for a second too long before it flickered to life—unnamed, unclaimed, blank except for the numbers blinking across the lock screen. She entered the code. Four digits. Muscle memory.

The phone unlocked.

And there it was, sent three days ago. One message, sitting quietly like a spider in the center of its web.

Room 604. I know what you did.

Her stomach dropped before her mind even registered the words. She read them again, slower this time - not because she didn't understand them, but because some part of her had always known this moment would come.

She powered down the phone and slipped it into the seam of her coat like a blade. Then she closed the drawer, slow and silent. The secret was hidden now, but the situation was still a coffin that wouldn't stay buried.

Upstairs, the house felt colder, as if whatever warmth had existed earlier had followed the girls out the door and taken the light with it. Claire walked the hallway without truly deciding to. Her feet moved as if summoned, not by memory, but by muscle — the body remembering what the mind had no interest in recalling.

Claire paused outside the guest bathroom. The mirror inside was small, square, framed in brushed nickel that had tarnished at the corners. She hadn't used it in months.

Inside the drawer beneath the sink — the third one down, where she kept bandages and cough drops - her fingers brushed something smooth and round. She didn't have to look. She knew the shape - a lipstick tube.

She drew it out slowly, held it in her palm like a relic, a confession, a dare.

The cap gave a soft click as it opened, and there it was: the shade she hadn't worn since her name had been different, since her smile had been a weapon and her body a stage.

Rapture.

Deep, red, defiant.

She turned toward the mirror. Her reflection met her eyes — softer now, but still hiding something beneath the surface.

Something sharp. She lifted the tube and, without breathing, pressed it to her lips.

Slowly, methodically, she applied it.

The woman in the mirror became someone else.

Not a wife. Not a mother. Not even Claire.

Someone older than the truth, but younger than the lie. Someone who had once stood in the hallway of a hotel suite with a purse full of cash and blood on her hands.

She stared at herself for a long time.

Then she wiped it away with a tissue, scrubbed until her lips stung. She flushed the tissue, washed her hands twice, and shut the drawer—harder than necessary.

But the face in the mirror lingered. And for one fractured second, she wasn't sure it would ever be gone.

…

The drive to Meredith's house felt both too long and not long enough, as if time had bent to accommodate the thoughts she was trying - and failing - to outrun. Claire gripped the steering wheel as if the smooth leather might anchor her, though her mind was adrift in that strange liminal space where nothing feels entirely real, where each intersection and passing sidewalk takes on the unreality of a stage set. When she turned into the tree-lined cul-de-sac and saw Meredith's pale brick house with its wreath still hanging on the front door despite the change in season, Claire felt something in her chest unclench, if only by an inch. Before she could knock, the door swung open.

"You must be psychic," Claire said, half smiling.

"Or just hopelessly nosy." Meredith grinned as she pulled her into a hug, one arm around her shoulders, the other resting briefly on the back of her neck, the way only people who really know you do. She smelled like lavender and rosemary and something faintly powdery, like warm fabric after a long shower.

Inside, the house was filled with soft light and the sound of Norah Jones humming gently from somewhere in the background. The kitchen counter was covered in a half made salad and an open bottle of wine—white, already breathing. Claire slid onto the stool she always used, the one near the window with the chip in the tile underneath.

"You want a glass?" Meredith asked.

"It's barely eleven."

"So? It's grape juice with ambition."

Claire laughed softly. The sound surprised her.

Meredith poured without waiting for permission and set the glass in front of her like it was medicine.

For a while, they didn't speak. Claire sipped. Meredith stirred something in a ceramic bowl with too much attention.

The air between them was the kind of quiet that came from close friendships—easy, unthreatening, intentional.

"You seem quiet," Meredith said finally, not accusing, just observing.

Claire turned the glass in her hand. "I'm just tired."

Meredith said nothing. Just waited.

Claire stared at the window, at the way the light fell in fractured lines across the wood floor. Then, quietly: "Do you ever feel like you've outrun something, only to realize it's been sitting in your passenger seat the whole time?"

Meredith blinked, but she said nothing, she just came around the counter and sat on the stool beside Claire, closer now, their knees almost touching. She reached over and gently brushed a loose strand of hair from Claire's cheek, tucking it behind her ear the way a sister might.

"I don't know what that means," she said softly, "but I know this—you are not alone. And whatever it is, whatever has you walking around like you're carrying a secret too heavy for one person... I'm here. You know that, right?"

Claire nodded, eyes burning.

"I mean it," Meredith whispered. "You don't have to say a word. I'll sit here with you in the dark if that's what you need. I'll stay until the lights come back on."

Claire reached for her hand and squeezed it, hard.

She allowed herself to imagine —really believe—that someone had her back.

The drive back was a quiet unraveling. No music. No podcast. Just the sound of tires on asphalt and the occasional hollow gust of wind against the windows, like something outside was trying to whisper its way in. Claire kept both hands on the wheel, her fingers tight against the leather, the bones of her knuckles standing out in the late-morning light.

Meredith's words echoed in her chest - I'll sit with you in the dark… I'll stay until the lights come back on.

Claire wanted to believe her. God, she wanted to. But belief didn't erase what was buried, and warmth couldn't cauterize a wound that refused to scab.

When she pulled into her driveway, she sat for a long time with the engine off, keys still dangling from the ignition. The sun was higher now, pouring in sideways through the windshield, casting her reflection faintly across the glass. Her face looked pale, her eyes older than they should have been. The lipstick was gone, scrubbed away with a tissue and a lie, and yet she could still feel it - the phantom heat of it on her mouth, the ghost of a woman who had once worn it like armor.

She climbed out of the car slowly. Her legs felt heavier than they had an hour ago. The weight of what she hadn't said, of what she'd let pass between her and Meredith without naming it, dragged behind her like a shadow stitched to her spine.

Inside, the house greeted her with its usual silence - not welcoming, not hostile. Just indifferent. Like it was waiting to see who she would be today.

Claire didn't take off her shoes. She left them on, laces still tied, tracked faint bits of the outside world across the floor as she moved through the entryway and into the kitchen, passing the dishwasher without looking at it, refusing to let her eyes even glance toward the place where the cup had been. She poured herself a glass of water and set it down on the counter without drinking it.

Then, almost automatically, she moved toward the pantry - a space not meant for retreat, but which had somehow become one.

She stepped inside and shut the door behind her, not all the way, just far enough that the outside dimmed and the shadows inside thickened around her. The shelves loomed quietly with their untouched cans and boxed broths and grains she kept buying but never cooked. She sat down on the low bench beneath the wire rack, pulling her knees up to her chest.

For a while, she didn't move. She just breathed. Listened to the house settle - the soft creak of something in the wall, the refrigerator's mechanical sigh, the vague hum of electricity threading through outlets like invisible veins. She'd once loved this house. Now it felt like a container for all the versions of herself she no longer recognized.

She reached into her coat pocket and pulled out the burner phone she had retrieved from the drawer in the kitchen earlier.

It was still powered down.

She hesitated, her thumb hovering over the button. Part of her wanted to throw it. Another part - the one that still knew how to hide behind locked doors and hotel aliases - told her she needed to know.

Always know.

She pressed the button.

The screen lit slowly, as though reluctant to wake.

The passcode screen blinked to life: four blank squares.

Her fingers entered the digits before she could stop them - a code no one else knew.

The phone unlocked.

Room 604. I know what you did.

The message stared back at her like it had teeth.

Claire swallowed, her throat dry and tight, her heart ticking louder than the silence around her. She read it twice, then a third time, as if repetition might dull its edge or make it more logical, less ominous, more… manageable.

It didn't.

Her thumbs hovered again. Then slowly, deliberately, she typed:

I don't do that anymore.

She hit send.

There was no reply.

Outside, the sun was beginning its slow descent, painting the driveway in long shadows. And across the street, partially obscured by the low-hanging branches of the oak tree, a car idled behind a soft veil of pollen and dust.

Dark. Tinted.

Motionless.

Chapter Two

The Box

Claire was already awake when the alarm went off.

She had been for hours—lying still beneath the duvet in the dark, her limbs arranged as if for a portrait, her eyes open but unfocused, and her thoughts folded so tightly in upon themselves they barely moved.

The quiet in her head had taken on an unnatural weight, the kind of silence that presses inward, compacting everything until it hums with pressure just beneath the surface.

The room was no longer still, not exactly; the heater clicked softly through the floor vents with a rhythm that might have been comforting on another day, and beside her, Mark's breath came in slow, indifferent waves, each exhale landing like an absence. He sounded far away. Tethered to a dream that had no room for her in it.

The sharp beep of the alarm punctured the dark, but she didn't startle. She silenced it before the second tone and slid from the bed with practiced ease, careful not to let the mattress sigh beneath her weight, not because she feared waking Mark—he never stirred when she left—but because silence had become a kind of ritual, a shield, and she respected its boundaries like sacred law.

She moved barefoot down the hallway, the skin of her soles barely whispering against the hardwood as she passed the girls' doors. Sadie's was cracked an inch, as always, her foot poking from under a pink blanket with stars. Emma's was nearly shut, earbuds still in from the night before, a lazy tendril of hair curled around the knob. Claire didn't pause. She kept going.

In the kitchen, the morning light was just beginning to bloom. Not golden, not yet, but that pre-dawn blue that softens the edges of everything and makes the world feel like it's holding its breath. It spilled through the windows like cool water, brushing against the cabinet fronts and stainless steel handles with quiet reverence, as if the house itself were reluctant to wake.

She filled the kettle with a steady hand, wiped the already clean counters for no reason except rhythm, and set the breakfast table with unconscious elegance—knife, fork, cloth napkin folded to a crisp rectangle beside Mark's coffee cup. She lined the strawberries up on a porcelain plate in a precise fan, then paused and removed one. Five was too many. Four looked deliberate. Symmetry mattered.

Claire had always been good at the performance of care.

She buttered toast without thinking, added jam that glistened like lacquer, poured juice with exactitude, turned the labels on the yogurt containers to face outward in the fridge. Her movements were graceful and unhurried, less like chores and more like ceremony. Each gesture a reassurance. Each line straightened, each mug rinsed, each drawer closed without sound. She had created a sanctuary from control— one that looked effortless from the outside, but only because every inch of it had been polished by fear.

Mark came down twenty minutes later, already dressed. His tie was perfect, the knot sharp and centered. His phone glowed in one hand, thumb scrolling without pause. He looked like a man pulled directly from a magazine ad for mid-tier mortgages—clean-cut, confident, just distracted enough to seem important.

"You're up early," he said without looking up.

Claire smiled—small, practiced, sweet. "Wanted to get a head start."

"Don't overdo it." He leaned down, pressed a kiss to her cheek that missed more than it landed, already halfway through an email. "You're not running for Wife of the Year."

She laughed softly. "Too late."

He didn't hear her. Or maybe he did and didn't care.

Emma and Sadie tumbled in next—Sadie barefoot, Emma half-braided, both wrapped in the sleepy chaos of their morning routine, arguing over whether Friday counted as a weekend if it began with a spelling test.

Claire knelt to tie Emma's shoes even though she could do it herself, tucked Sadie's curls behind her ear, handed out chewable vitamins and perfectly browned toast slices like a hostess at a brunch no one had asked for but everyone expected.

"I left your thermos in your backpack," she told Mark, brushing crumbs from the table. "And your charger's in the car."

He nodded, distracted again. "Knew I forgot something."

She didn't say anything about how forgetful he usually was. About how much of the household he floated above like a guest. She just smiled again, thin and automatic, and leaned back against the counter as the scene unfolded before her— her family moving through the motions like actors in a scene she had directed. It was flawless in its choreography. Almost believable in its warmth.

She waited until the girls had left for the bus stop—Emma with her hoodie pulled over one earbud and a lazy wave, Sadie still chattering about the injustice of education—and Mark had backed out of the driveway with a quick double beep and a glance at his mirror.

Only then did she sit. Not just perch briefly the way she often did between tasks, but sit with weight, her hands resting like dormant things in her lap, her back curving into the chair like she no longer trusted her own spine to hold her.

The house was quiet now, but not peacefully so. The silence wasn't relief—it was recoil. A hush with teeth.

She hadn't eaten. She rarely did when her nerves coiled this tightly, when the pulse at the base of her throat felt like a live wire just beneath the skin. Food tasted like cardboard when fear bloomed under her tongue. She had made breakfast for everyone else, of course. Sliced fruit with precision. Toasted the bread just to the edge of crisp. Folded napkins into squares that didn't collapse. She had done it all perfectly, the way a good wife should. The way a better mother must.

But now, alone, her stomach felt like a closed fist.

She stood too quickly. Her knees wobbled, and the movement brought a bloom of static to the edges of her vision—a flash of white that reminded her of camera flashes or a memory too bright to look at directly. She braced

herself against the counter, palms flat against the marble, until the world steadied itself again.

Instinct took over. She cleaned things that didn't need cleaning—fingertips grazing along baseboards, fluffing pillows already puffed, folding the living room throw blanket into corners so sharp they looked machine-pressed. She found a sock beneath the couch and held it like a relic, unsure if she was solving a mystery or simply stalling the one unraveling around her.

And then—

The doorbell rang.

She froze mid-step. Her breath hitched and held. It was too early for deliveries. She wasn't expecting anything.

Meredith wouldn't ring the bell—she always let herself in with a melodic hum and a familiarity that never knocked.

Claire moved toward the door like she was approaching a sleeping predator—deliberate, measured, as if each step might trigger something she couldn't undo.

She opened it.

No one stood there.

No shadow retreating down the porch. No clipboard wielding teen with a package. Just air. And a single, small box.

Brown. Unbranded. Placed dead center on the welcome mat like an accusation.

Her eyes swept the street. A dark-colored car turned the corner two blocks down—too fast to catch a license plate, too slow to be dismissed. It disappeared with no brake lights. No indication of where it had come from or where it was going.

She stepped outside barefoot, the chill of the porch stone sharp against her soles, and picked up the package with both hands—holding it not like a delivery, but like a threat.

Inside, in the kitchen, she set it gently on the island and stared.

There was no label. No return address. No barcode. No stamps.

This hadn't come through any official channel. It had been delivered—*placed.* By someone who knew where she lived. Someone who knew she'd be the one to find it. Someone who wanted her to know it had never been about coincidence.

She opened the drawer slowly, retrieved the scissors, and hesitated for a moment—long enough to count a breath she didn't remember taking.

Then she sliced the tape with one clean motion.

The box opened with a sigh.

Inside was a single item.

A hotel key card.

Worn plastic. White, with a black magnetic stripe. The faint logo of the **Mason Hill Hotel and Conference Center** nearly rubbed away, as though it had spent years in someone's wallet, passed through fingers over and over like a worry stone.

Claire didn't move. Her lungs emptied with such sudden force it felt like drowning. She stared at it—unblinking, unbreathing—as her mind tried to reject what her body already knew.

Room 604.

She had thrown it away. She had watched it fall into the metal trash bin in a gas station bathroom three towns away, buried it under wet paper towels and crumpled receipts. She had *let it go.*

But here it was.

In her kitchen.

On her table.

She didn't touch it. Not with bare hands. Not yet.

She opened the cabinet beneath the kitchen sink and pulled out the pair of long, pale gloves she used for bleach and oven cleaner—rubber, slightly powdery, the insides cool against her skin. Her movements were precise, mechanical. Reverent, almost. She slipped them on with care, as though the act of covering her hands could also shield the parts of her memory she hadn't invited back in.

Then she picked up the key card with gloved fingers, careful not to let it touch her skin, and walked upstairs—each step deliberate, as though the act of moving through the house required negotiation with every floorboard.

In the bedroom closet, behind the row of heavy winter coats she hadn't worn in months, she pulled down a plain, unmarked shoebox. Inside were two items: the lipstick stained teacup, the dishwasher wasn't able to cut through the sticky red wax, and the burner phone. She placed the key card beside them—three relics of a life she thought she'd buried—and closed the lid. Then she pushed the box deep into the corner of her closet.

She let the coats fall back into place, the thick wool sleeves brushing the box like curtains closing on a secret performance no one had paid to see. For a long moment, she didn't move. She just stood in the shadowed closet, her hands empty, her pulse soft and shallow. The air inside the closet was stale with forgotten things—old boots, off-season scarves, the faint trace of cedar from a sachet she'd tucked on a shelf years ago and never replaced. Everything dormant. Everything buried. Except the part of her that now thrummed beneath the surface like a wire pulled too tight.

When she finally moved, it was with a strange lightness, as though her body had remembered the choreography even while her mind stood frozen on the edge of the stage.

She walked back downstairs. The house had settled again, in that eerie, unnatural hush it always seemed to adopt when she was alone. The kind of quiet that didn't soothe, didn't rest, didn't ease—but waited.

She had just reached the bottom step when the sound came: the clean, sure click of a key in the front door.

Not the uncertain rattle of someone testing locks, but the smooth, practiced turn of someone who belonged—or believed they did.

She didn't flinch.

Instead, she exhaled the breath she hadn't known she was holding and allowed her body to move again. The tension that had wrapped itself around her spine like thread loosened just enough to let her shoulders fall.

And then she heard elegant, jazzy humming.

Soft and unhurried, shapeless and tuneless, the sort of melody that had no real beginning and no end. It floated in with the opening of the door like it belonged to the house itself.

Meredith.

"Claire?" came the call, light and sing-song. "Please tell me you're not elbows-deep in grout or reorganizing the spice rack alphabetically again. I brought scones. You're required by law to sit down and eat at least one."

Claire let the breath slip from her chest and shaped her voice around a smile. "In here."

Meredith appeared in the kitchen doorway moments later, the scent of bakery sugar trailing behind her, a canvas tote in one hand and a cardboard pastry box in the other. Her copper-red curls framed her face in soft, effortless spirals that made her look both younger and more composed than she probably felt. Her coat was unbuttoned, her cheeks pink from the cold. She always entered like she belonged—like the space had been waiting just for her.

She took one look at Claire and her expression shifted, softened. "You didn't sleep."

Claire opened her mouth to protest, but Meredith had already crossed to the cabinet, pulled two plates, and began unpacking the pastries like a woman on a mission. She filled the kettle with practiced ease and retrieved the very mugs Claire hadn't realized she'd set out earlier.

"You don't have to—" Claire began.

Meredith cut her off gently. "I want to."

They sat together at the island, the scones between them, steam curling upward from their mugs like breath in cold air. Claire picked at the corner of one with absent fingers, tearing it piece by piece but not yet tasting it. The smell reminded her of some other morning—some other kitchen—though she couldn't name which. Just warmth. And cinnamon. And distraction.

"You okay?" Meredith asked, tilting her head.

Claire nodded. Too fast.

"Fine," she said. "Just tired."

"You've been tired for months."

Claire tried to smile. It didn't hold.

"I'm managing."

"You don't have to keep managing. You're allowed to fall apart. You know that, right?"

Claire stared into her tea. "If I stop holding it all together, who's going to clean up the mess?"

Meredith's hand came to rest lightly on hers. Not urgent. Not pitying. Just present. Solid.

"Then let me be the one who catches it," she said. "Whatever it is. I'm here."

Claire swallowed. "Thank you."

Meredith smiled gently. "You'd do the same for me."

Claire returned the smile. And for a moment—just long enough to feel dangerous—she believed it.

They sat in silence, sipping tea, letting the world drift at its own pace beyond the kitchen windows. Claire hadn't felt that kind of stillness in weeks.

Later, after Meredith had gone—after her perfume had faded from the air and the last crumbs had been brushed into the sink—Claire stepped outside. The sky was a dull, pewter gray, low and pressing, the kind of winter cloud cover that flattened everything into one long, waiting breath. The air was too still. No wind. No birds. Just cold.

She walked slowly to the mailbox, her steps even, unconcerned. Her sweater sleeves pulled down over her wrists. Her hands only loosely curled around the junk mail and bills. She wasn't expecting anything unusual. She hadn't ordered anything. Still, she looked both ways out of habit.

That's when she saw it.

A car.

Parked two houses down. Not in anyone's driveway. Not at the curb like it belonged. Just still. Idle. Engine on, barely. Windows tinted dark enough to hide the shape of the driver.

She didn't stop. Didn't run. Didn't stare.

She walked back toward the house, posture calm, steps steady, breathing quiet but too shallow. The key turned in the lock with a small, mechanical click, and when the door closed behind her, she stood there for a full minute before engaging the deadbolt.

The house seemed darker than before. Or maybe it was just the cloud cover. Or the car. Or the way fear settled into a room like smoke—slow at first, then choking.

Then the phone rang.

The landline. An analog sound that cracked against the quiet like glass.

She moved toward it, hand already reaching, her eyes scanning the caller ID. Unknown number.

She picked up. "Hello?"

"Mrs. Holloway?" a woman's voice asked, professional but not warm. "This is Nurse Kellerman from Oakridge Elementary. I just wanted to let you know that Sadie came to the health office after lunch. She says she has a headache and seemed a bit flushed."

Claire straightened. "Is she running a fever?"

"Not at the moment. It might just be fatigue or dehydration, but she looked a little pale. She's resting now, but I told her we'd call you anyway."

Claire nodded instinctively, though no one could see her. "I'll come get her. Thank you."

She hung up without a pause and stood very still for a moment, her reflection barely visible in the black screen of the microwave. It was always like this—one thing after another, layering like fine dust over a life she could barely see through anymore. One small crack in the day, and suddenly everything felt brittle again.

She made her way upstairs slowly, changed out of her loungewear and into jeans and a cashmere sweater—both soft, neutral, flattering. The kind of outfit that said I'm doing fine without requiring her to say anything at all. She pulled her hair back, applied just enough concealer to erase the insomnia, and checked the doors and windows twice before leaving the house.

The car door closed with a gentle thud. Her hands stayed at ten and two. Everything routine. Everything right.

And yet—her eyes flicked to the rearview mirror.

The street looked normal. The shadows fell where they should. No car trailed behind her.

But still, she felt it—that prickle at the base of her neck. Like her name was being spoken in a room she couldn't see.

Claire pulled into the circular drive at Oakridge Elementary a few minutes after one, the sun caught just behind a veil of clouds, leaving everything bathed in a pale silver light that made the brick building seem colder, quieter than usual. A few children milled near the office doors, escorted by teachers or aides, but the playground was empty—too late for recess, too early for dismissal.

She parked, stepped out, and adjusted the hem of her sweater with one hand, smoothing it as if it might flatten something inside her. Her heels clicked softly on the concrete as she walked up the ramp and into the office, where the secretary offered her a brief smile and waved her toward the nurse's door.

Sadie sat curled on a plastic cot in the corner of the dimly lit health room, her small frame blanketed in one of the thin navy throws the school kept for emergencies. She looked up when Claire entered, her face pale and slightly puffy, her lower lip tucked between her teeth in a familiar way that made Claire's heart fracture just a little.

"Hi, sweet girl," Claire said gently, kneeling beside the cot. "You don't look so good."

Sadie shrugged, her voice faint. "My head hurts. I didn't eat all my lunch."

Claire smoothed a hand across her daughter's forehead, not because she expected to feel fever, but because she needed the contact—needed the proof of her daughter's presence in this world, in this moment, alive and breathing and vulnerable.

"Let's go home," she whispered. "We'll do something quiet. Maybe hot cocoa and that drawing book you like?"

Sadie nodded, nestling into her mother's side for just a second before pulling the blanket off and sliding into her shoes. Claire helped her gather her things, smiled and thanked Nurse Kellerman, and held her daughter's hand all the way to the car.

As they drove, Claire stole glances in the rearview mirror. Not at the street this time, but at her child's face—soft and tired, a little flushed but smiling now as she hummed quietly to herself, a loose strand of hair caught in her lashes, her thumb resting near her mouth the way it had when she was three.

Her backpack lay crumpled at her side, one strap dangling across her lap.

She wanted to reach back. To offer her hand. To let Sadie know, in some unspoken way, that she was safe. But instead, she simply glanced into the mirror again, met her daughter's sleepy gaze, and smiled.

And for that brief stretch of road, she let herself believe that everything might still be okay.

Chapter Three

The Photo

The envelope had not been there the night before. Claire was certain of it.

She had locked the door herself after Mark came home from the gym—double-checked the bolt out of habit, then lingered in the kitchen longer than she needed to, watching the glow from the under-cabinet lights shimmer against the quartz counters, listening to the familiar hum of the refrigerator and the slow, meditative clink of the dishwasher finishing its cycle. It had been quiet then, late and still, the kind of hush that settles only when the whole house has finally exhaled. She'd stood there, barefoot, arms crossed loosely over her chest, staring at nothing in particular. The floor had been clean. Empty. She would have noticed. She always noticed.

But now, as morning light curled softly across the hardwood and the faint drone of cartoons floated from behind closed bedroom doors upstairs—punctuated by the occasional burst of Sadie's laughter and Emma's third request for more strawberries—there it was. Slim. Pale. Perfectly still. A white envelope positioned just beneath the lip of the doorframe, slightly off-center, like it had hesitated before committing. As though it hadn't been placed but had instead crept into the room on its own, crossing a boundary it wasn't meant to pass.

No name. No handwriting. No stamp. Just a single, silent white envelope—plain, almost sterile, and yet so jarringly out of place that it seemed to hum with threat. This wasn't something left on the porch or forgotten beneath a stack of mail. It was slipped inside deliberately. Inside her house. Inside the sealed, locked quiet of her home. A violation posing as something benign.

Sadie's laughter still tumbled down the staircase now and then in cheerful bursts, and Emma had already asked for more strawberries twice—but even so, in Claire's mind, there was a strange, deliberate hush pressed around the envelope. A silence that wasn't about sound, but about energy. As though the air itself had receded. As though time had paused in deference to whatever that thing was, lying there like a planted seed of dread. Her body was alert, every muscle drawn tight in its stillness, her mind flickering through rational explanations and discarding them just as quickly. There was no natural place in her morning for this. And yet—it was here. Unavoidable. Unwelcome.

When she finally bent to retrieve it, she did so with the kind of caution usually reserved for touching something living— fragile, reactive, possibly dangerous. Her fingers slid beneath the paper as if testing its temperature, lifting it slowly, gently, as though even the slightest sudden movement might trigger something irreversible. The flap opened without resistance, no adhesive, no seal—just an invitation, or a dare, disguised in stationery. Her pulse thudded in her ears as the envelope parted, her breath held not from fear, but from the terrible certainty that whatever was inside would change the shape of the day entirely. Of everything.

Inside was a single black-and-white photograph.

No note. No explanation. Just the image—grainy and harsh, rendered in that washed-out, surveillance-grade contrast that made everything look colder than it was. The kind of photo printed on cheap thermal stock, the ink already ghosting at the edges, but unmistakably real. The timestamp in the upper corner caught her eye first—red digital numbers, precise and pitiless. Claire didn't have to do the math. She knew that date. She knew that hallway. Her gaze trailed down the printed image, her breath locked in place as she found the patterned carpet, the blurred sconce lights, the metal digits affixed to the door.

604.

Her stomach twisted, an instinctive clench that pulled her center downward.

A figure stood mid-step in the center of the frame, caught in the act of slipping through the door as though frozen in time by some silent, mechanical witness. The coat was cinched tightly at the waist, familiar in its shape and slope. The hair—dark, pulled back—tucked beneath a cheap synthetic wig. The face obscured by angle and blur, but the posture… that was unmistakable. Claire felt it in her spine before her brain caught up. She remembered the weight of that coat, the way the belt always knotted to the left. She remembered the way she'd walked that night—quick, careful, not hurried but practiced. It was her. The camera hadn't caught her face, but it had caught enough. Too much.

She remembered the wig. The one she always wore for protection—for separation. A fragile veil of anonymity that made her feel like someone else entirely, someone untouchable, invisible. She was blonde, naturally, with ice blue eyes that people often mistook for pretty rather than sharp. But for appointments, she'd worn a dark wig and green contact lenses—just enough of a transformation to keep Delia separate from Claire, just enough to feel like she was slipping into armor. That small barrier was all that had kept her safe until now. It was the only reason her name hadn't surfaced, the only reason her door hadn't been knocked on sooner. She stared at the figure in the photo, at her own shape made foreign by grayscale distortion, and felt a flicker of vertigo—like looking into a mirror that reflected not her face, but her secret.

She turned the photo over with deliberate care, her fingertips precise, already bracing herself for what might be waiting on the other side. A threat. A signature. A name. But there was no flourish, no context—just five stark words etched in thin, mechanical typeface, the kind of ink that looked almost too faint to matter. And yet, the message rang louder than a scream:

You didn't stay hidden long.

No punctuation. No handwriting. Just a cold observation delivered without emotion. And that was what made it most dangerous.

The photograph was folded once—cleanly, silently—and slid into the spine of a cookbook no one touched anymore. The kind with yellowed pages and outdated measurements, a relic from another version of her life. Claire's movements were smooth, unhurried, practiced. She tucked it behind newer cookbooks she never used, arranging them just so, creating the illusion of untouched order. No sharp gestures. No panic. Just the steady grace of a woman refusing to give anything away. She poured herself coffee. She opened the blinds. She moved through the morning like an actress in a scene she'd rehearsed a thousand times. And all the while, the aftershock trembled beneath her skin.

The knock came at 9:03.

Not frantic, not casual—three firm, evenly spaced raps against the door that echoed just slightly too loud in the quiet morning. Claire froze mid-step, coffee cup hovering beneath her mouth, the steam curling up unnoticed. Her mind leapt ahead, running possibilities like a film reel on fast-forward.

Mark was out on his run. The girls were upstairs in their pajamas with trays of breakfast and their favorite movies, their laughter floating down like a lullaby. No deliveries were expected. No friends were stopping by. Which meant… this was something else. Something outside the script.

She set the mug down with care, the ceramic clicking softly against the counter, and walked to the door with a composure that belied the pulse hammering beneath her skin. Each step was measured, her face schooled into a neutral calm, her breath shallow but controlled. She opened the door just wide enough to see him. A man stood on the porch—late forties, clean-shaven, his blazer sharp but unremarkable. His posture was relaxed but alert, the stance of someone used to being let in. Claire's gaze caught on the glint of metal clipped inside his jacket. A badge. He reached into his pocket and withdrew a folded leather wallet, flipping it open with practiced ease.

"Mrs. Holloway?" His voice was calm, professional, measured to reassure. "Detective Ray Hollis. I was hoping to ask you a few questions. May I?"

Claire didn't move to widen the door. Her body remained angled against the frame—neither fully blocking his view nor inviting him in. A calculated posture. Her expression hovered somewhere between polite confusion and mild concern, the kind of practiced neutrality that made people underestimate her. "What's this about?" she asked, her tone even, almost bored. But inside, the walls of her chest had drawn tight.

"It's in regard to an incident that occurred last year at the Mason Hill Hotel and Conference Suites," he said, watching her closely. "Room 604. A man named David Halbrook was found deceased. We've reopened some inquiries."

The name landed like a stone dropped in still water. Claire didn't blink. But inside, something flinched. A long pause stretched between them—too long to be casual, too short to be suspicious—and she allowed herself a single breath, shallow and controlled. "I'm afraid I don't know anyone by that name," she said, her voice smooth as glass.

Hollis nodded once, the gesture unreadable. "Understood. We're just following up on a list of contacts found in Mr. Holbrook's phone records. Your number and address were saved. No context—just a name. Claire Holloway."

She tilted her head slightly, as if processing something strange but ultimately inconsequential. Her brow furrowed— just enough. "That's… odd. I wish I could be more helpful."

Her voice didn't waver. Not even slightly. But a distant, warning thrum had started up behind her ribs. Her name.

Her address. On his phone. No context, he'd said. But the context, of course, was everything.

"Of course. It may be nothing," Hollis said, the corners of his mouth pulling into a faint, polite smile that didn't reach his eyes. "But in cases like this, we like to speak to everyone connected to the decedent, however loosely. Just to be thorough."

He held her gaze evenly, but there was a subtle weight behind his words—a kind of quiet implication that made Claire's spine stiffen. His tone remained cordial, professional, but there was a question buried beneath every syllable. One he hadn't asked aloud. One he didn't need to.

Claire met his eyes, letting the moment hang there—just long enough to seem thoughtful, but not evasive. Then she offered a mild, almost apologetic shrug. "I'm sure it's just a coincidence. Wrong number, maybe. There are a lot of Claire Holloways."

It was the kind of response that offered nothing and asked nothing in return. Perfectly neutral. Utterly forgettable. And yet, she could feel the thrum of unease tightening behind her ribs, steady as a metronome. He hadn't come for nothing. And he wasn't leaving with nothing, either.

Hollis didn't press. "Possibly," he said, slipping back into the polite cadence of someone closing a file. "I appreciate your time, Mrs. Holloway." He reached into his jacket and pulled out a card, holding it between two fingers like an afterthought. "If anything comes to mind—anything at all—please don't hesitate to reach out. My number's on the back."

Claire took it with a feather-light touch, nodding once. "Of course."

The exchange was ordinary in every visible way. But beneath it, something cold and deliberate unspooled.

The detective stepped back from the porch, pausing only to give her a final glance over his shoulder. "Go well, Missy," he said, with a half-smile that felt more like a test than a farewell.

Claire closed the door quietly. Locked it. Then stood there, her palm still pressed to the knob, the metal cooling beneath her touch as if the heat of the moment had only just begun to fade. Her pulse wasn't racing—but something deeper had shifted. Not panic, not yet. But the unmistakable tightening of a snare she'd almost forgotten was wrapped around her ankle.

She glanced toward the neat row of recipe books. The photograph might not be enough. Not yet. But it had started something. Stirred the air. Marked the perimeter of her safety with new, invisible lines. And now, the police were knocking. Not metaphorically. Not theoretically. Actually.

She turned the deadbolt with the same automatic rhythm she used for brushing her teeth or setting the table—an act so rehearsed it had become muscle memory. But today, it felt like something more. A ritual. A closing ceremony.

The scent of maple syrup still hung in the air, sweet and cloying, as if breakfast hadn't fully released its grip on the house. Upstairs, the high-pitched jingle of a cartoon theme song drifted through the stairwell—bright, chirpy, almost manic in its cheerfulness. Claire stood in the hush beneath it all, the domestic rhythm still ticking around her like a windup toy, steady and oblivious. But the calm was surface level. Underneath, something had shifted. Her hand slipped from the door, and her feet moved with quiet intent toward the hallway. Toward the stairs. Toward her closet.

The box was still there.

She hadn't checked yet, but somehow she knew. It was the kind of certainty that lived in the body, not the mind—a low, thrumming instinct that said: nothing's been touched, but everything's changed. She moved up the stairs, each step deliberate, her hand grazing the wall as she ascended. At the top, she turned toward the bedroom,and slipped inside without turning on the light. The closet door creaked faintly as she opened it. Behind the winter coats—buried deep, where only she would think to reach—a shoebox waited in the dark.

She crouched down and pulled it toward her, the cardboard soft at the corners from years of handling, its lid slightly bowed. Nothing about it looked remarkable. It could have held old photos, baby shoes, outgrown gloves. But inside, it held the things she hadn't yet found the courage to destroy— the artifacts of another life. She lifted the lid and looked down at the contents, arranged not with sentiment, but with precision. The burner phone, powered off. The lipstick stained cup, wrapped once in paper towel. And the key card from the Mason Hill Hotel and Conference Center.

The three items seemed to hum in the dark, charged with a quiet energy that didn't belong in a suburban closet. She stared down at them, as if by arranging them just so she might make sense of their presence, of what they meant now. Not just objects. Not just remnants. Warnings. Messages. A breadcrumb trail left by someone who knew exactly who she used to be—and wanted her to remember.

Her fingers hovered above the key card for several seconds, as if touching it might collapse the distance between then and now. She remembered the way it had clicked in the door.

The brief, metallic whir. The moment she had hesitated in the hallway, coat pulled tight, heart pounding with something that was not yet dread. Her hand moved closer, then pulled back. She didn't want to touch it without gloves.

Didn't want her skin on it again. Not now. Not after the photo. Not after the Detective had come knocking.

She let her mind go back to that night.

Room 604. The room where everything changed. Where she had a disagreement with her client. When he'd started getting mad she had stepped out to take a call. David Holbrook had died on the carpet just minutes later. Her name was never supposed to be known. But David had found it. And someone else had found her.

She closed the lid to the box quickly, her bare hands trembling just slightly as the cardboard met itself with a soft thud. She didn't want to look anymore. The sight of those objects—so small, so ordinary—felt unbearable now, like relics dredged up from a life she no longer claimed. She didn't want to remember. Not the hallway. Not the hotel. Not the silence after the fall. She wanted it all to disappear, to vanish beneath the winter coats and the weight of denial. But memory had a pulse of its own—and hers was starting to beat louder.

She slid the box back into place, deep beneath the coats—thick wool, heavy knits, the kind of layers no one would need until December. It disappeared easily, swallowed by folds of fabric and shadow. Claire stood and shut the closet door, her hand lingering on the knob for a moment longer than necessary. It felt like closing a vault. A weak one. She knew it wouldn't hold forever.

She moved through the bedroom in silence, her feet soundless on the hardwood, her breath steady but shallow. In the mirror above her dresser, she caught her own reflection—shoulders drawn, eyes too wide, skin pale beneath the morning light. Blonde. Ice blue. That's who she really was. Not the dark-haired, green-eyed woman who used to walk hotel hallways in four-inch heels and anonymity. That woman had been a mask, a necessity. But sometimes Claire wondered which version of herself had been more real.

She turned away from the mirror, refusing to let that question take root. Down the hall, a door creaked open, followed by the patter of small feet and the clink of something plastic—probably Sadie's cereal bowl on the floor again. Claire listened, letting the sound anchor her. This life was real. This house, these daughters, the steady thrum of ordinary things. She had built it all from scratch, one careful decision at a time. But lately, it felt as if someone had started pulling at the seams.

She stepped into the hallway and pulled the bedroom door closed behind her, slow and soundless. The scent of syrup still hung faintly in the air, mingling with the crispness of freshly laundered sheets and the distant hum of the dishwasher downstairs. Everything looked the same. Everything felt… off. Like a stage set she was suddenly too aware of, the edges too perfect, the props too still. She descended the stairs with the practiced ease of someone who had done it a thousand times—but now, each step carried weight. Not just her own. Something else. Something watching.

In the kitchen, she moved to the sink and rinsed out a half empty juice glass left from breakfast, watching the water swirl and vanish. The hum of the refrigerator seemed louder than usual, the kind of mechanical drone that filled the silence when no one dared speak. On the island, the detective's card remained untouched—its presence quiet but insistent, like something ticking. She didn't reach for it.

Instead, she opened the fridge, staring at rows of condiments and leftover pasta, letting the cool air fog her thoughts. She needed a plan. She needed time. But most of all, she needed to stay invisible.

She crossed to the back door and checked the lock, then the window above the sink, then the side entrance—movements rehearsed, automatic, but today tinged with something else. Not fear exactly. Not yet. But vigilance. A sense that the world outside the glass had turned sharper overnight. She didn't expect to see anyone standing there. And no one was. But still, she checked. Twice.

She turned from the window and made her way back toward the stairs, pausing only briefly by the kitchen island. The detective's card lay where she'd left it, the inked name facing up like a dare. She didn't want to touch it again, but she couldn't leave it out—not with the girls around. With two fingers, she picked it up and slipped it into the side pocket of her handbag, which still hung from the hook by the door like it always did. Out of sight, for now. But close. Too close.

The kitchen radio crackled to life.
No one had touched it. No one had even been near it. But suddenly, the old speaker above the counter hissed with static, then caught a burst of warped music—some forgotten jingle twisting faintly before vanishing into silence again.

Claire froze, one hand still on the lock, her pulse thudding hard in her throat. The radio hadn't worked properly in years.

And then Emma screamed.

It wasn't a sharp, panicked sound—more a startled cry, high pitched and urgent. Claire's body snapped to attention, the air gone from her lungs before her feet were even moving.

She bounded up the remaining steps and threw open Emma's door.

Emma sat on her bed, wide-eyed but unharmed, the television frozen on some glitchy cartoon frame. "I—I didn't do anything," Emma stammered, clutching the remote like a weapon. "It just—froze. Then it made this weird, scary sound. like someone whispering my name."

Claire crossed the room in two strides, her hand brushing her daughter's hair back, her other hand steadying the screen as if that would fix it.

"It's okay," she whispered, breathless. "It's okay. Just a glitch."

But her hands were trembling.

Because it hadn't been the scream that scared her most.

It was the sudden, unmistakable feeling that someone had wanted her to hear it.

Claire stayed there for a moment, crouched beside the bed, her hand resting lightly on Emma's back. The screen buzzed faintly, the image frozen in a distorted grimace—some brightly colored character paused mid-expression, eyes too wide, smile twisted just enough to be wrong. Claire reached forward and turned the television off. The silence that followed wasn't comforting. It was expectant.

Emma looked up at her. "Why did it do that?"

"I don't know," Claire said softly. "Maybe the signal dropped. Or too much time on pause."

She stood and kissed the top of Emma's head. "It's fine now."

But her stomach had tightened into a hard knot.

Because something in that moment hadn't felt like a glitch. It had felt… staged

Claire left Emma's room with a soft click of the door and crossed the hall, pausing outside Sadie's. The glow of the tablet lit the edges of the darkened doorway, the faint murmur of animation voices rising and falling like a tide. She didn't step inside. Just stood there for a moment, listening. Making sure the rhythm of their world still pulsed.

Then she went back downstairs.

The house had the hush of late morning now—sunlight shifting across the floors, dishwasher ticking softly behind its final cycle. Everything in place. Everything calm. But her skin buzzed.

She glanced at the door—locked. Checked the side window—clear. But then she saw it.

Something barely visible.

Pressed flat beneath the welcome mat, just the corner of it peeking out. White. Thin.

Another envelope.

Claire didn't move at first. Her breath caught. Her hands, finally still. The walls felt too narrow, the silence too deep.

She reached for it slowly, sliding the envelope free with careful fingers. No markings. No stamp.

Inside was a single item.

A matchbook. Cream-colored. Embossed with deep green lettering.

MASON HILL HOTEL & CONFERENCE CENTER.

The same one. The same place. Room 604.

Claire stood there, the weight of it pinched between her fingers, as though holding it too long might ignite something she couldn't put out.

Because this wasn't a warning.

This was a reminder.

And whoever left it knew exactly where she'd been.

Chapter Four

The Stranger

It wasn't often that Claire left the house alone on a Saturday. But that afternoon, as the sunlight softened across the tops of the maples and the girls retreated into their own little weekend rituals—Emma with her earbuds and sketchbook, Sadie with her cartoons and sticky hands—Claire slipped

her purse over her shoulder and told Mark she'd run to the store.

He barely looked up from his phone. "You'll be gone…long?"

She shrugged. "An hour or so. Just a few things."

He gave a noncommittal grunt, which she took as permission. Lately, most of their conversations had collapsed into monosyllables and tones—what wasn't said weighed more than what was.

The grocery store was a few miles away, tucked into a plaza with the same predictable collection of suburban comforts: nail salon, dry cleaner, Pilates studio. Familiar. Safe. Or so it had always seemed.

Inside, the air conditioning hit her like a slap—overzealous and sterile. Claire grabbed a basket instead of a cart, not intending to buy much. A few things for dinner. Apples for the girls' lunches, maybe some ice cream for dessert.

Something to make it look like she was living a life that required ice cream.

She moved through the store slowly, enjoying the small luxury of being alone, unnoticed—or so she thought.

But then it began.

The looks.

Two women by the deli—both moms from Sadie's old preschool—offered her thin smiles, their eyes scanning her outfit a little too carefully. Claire was wearing a pale blue linen blouse tucked into tailored jeans and flats, no makeup except for a dab of tinted lip balm, but somehow they still looked at her as though she were trying too hard.

Or not hard enough.

Another woman, this one near the bakery, did a double take when she recognized her. "Claire, hi!" she chirped. "Oh my gosh, you look amazing."

Claire smiled politely, the way one does when offered a compliment wrapped in thin plastic. The woman's tone was too bright, her eyes too quick as they swept over Claire's blouse, her skin, her shoes. Claire could feel it—the effort to sound gracious, the envy leaking through the seams.

She moved toward the produce section, feeling the weight of eyes on her shoulders as she picked through a bin of Honey crisp apples. Her fingers trembled slightly. The performative nature of suburbia was exhausting.

"Claire?"

The voice came from behind her, male, unfamiliar in tone but with a faint edge of recognition that made her stomach twist.

She turned.

A man stood a few feet away, holding a bag of lemons. Late thirties, maybe forty. He looked normal in a bland, catalog sort of way—navy shirt, khakis, brown loafers, and an oversized sports jacket. He tugged at the brim of his baseball cap nervously. He wasn't unattractive, but forgettable. Except for the way he looked at her.

Like he knew her.

Intimately.

"Sorry," she said, her voice cooler than she intended. "Do I know you?"

He smiled, but it was tight, more of a stretch than a gesture. "I think so. Or—I did, once. A while back. You look exactly the same."

Claire gripped the apple in her hand, skin prickling beneath her sleeves. "I'm sorry, I'm not placing you."

His smile didn't fade. It just… stayed. "No worries. Must've been years ago. You were going by a different name then, I think."

Her breath hitched so quickly she nearly dropped the fruit. "Excuse me?" she said, her voice low and tight, more blade than breath.

The man just smiled—unbothered, almost amused, as if they were sharing an inside joke only he remembered.

"Forget it," he said. "I'm probably wrong."

She stared at him for a beat longer, her heart thudding now, heavy and unmistakable.

He turned casually, his movements unnervingly slow, and walked away.

"Go well, Missy," he said, as if the entire interaction had been a harmless mistake. As if he hadn't just cracked open the ground beneath her feet.

Claire stood frozen, unsure if her face had flushed or drained entirely. Her hand still clutched the apple, her fingers

digging into the skin. She looked around. No one else had heard. No one was watching. Just the hum of fluorescent lights and the casual oblivion of other shoppers.

That "stranger" had known her.

Or at least, he'd said enough to make her believe he did. "You were going by a different name then."

There was no possible way he could've said that by accident. No stranger would phrase it that way. Not unless he knew something. Not unless he knew about *Delia*.

Her first instinct was to leave—get out, now, before he circled back, before someone else saw her unraveling in front of the oranges. But another instinct, one born of years of curated poise, rooted her to the floor. She didn't move. Couldn't. Her mind was sprinting, but her body was frozen, pinned under a thousand invisible eyes.

A woman brushed past her with a cart full of juice boxes and granola bars, offering a bright, empty smile. Claire managed to nod in return, barely. The woman didn't seem to notice anything was wrong. No one did.

She turned, finally, and scanned the aisle. The man was gone. Vanished between displays of potatoes and bell peppers, or maybe down the cold cavern of the frozen food section. Gone, like he'd never been there at all. Like he'd slipped through the cracks in reality and taken her certainty with him.

Claire left her basket behind. Abandoned the apples. Walked briskly through the store, each step louder in her ears than the last. She passed a group of teenagers gathered near the energy drinks, a toddler shrieking over cereal, an elderly man arguing with a self-checkout screen.

Normal things. Loud things. Innocent things.

But her body didn't believe in normal anymore.

As she pushed through the sliding doors and stepped into the heavy, humid dusk of early evening, her breath finally returned to her in ragged pulls. The sky above was bruised with soft lavender clouds, the parking lot a flickering patchwork of brake lights and swarming gnats.

She unlocked her car with a trembling hand, slid into the driver's seat, and slammed the door harder than she intended. It was only then—enclosed, alone—that her hands truly began to shake.

She didn't start the engine. Just sat there, staring at the steering wheel, the world tilting slightly sideways.

A different name.
He'd said it like it was casual. Like it didn't carry the weight of a buried identity. Of a life she had smothered beneath layer after layer of normal.

Was it a coincidence? A threat? A mistake?

Or was she finally being found?

She closed her eyes, leaning her head back against the headrest, and tried to breathe. One second at a time.

She didn't drive straight home.

As her car rolled out of the lot, Claire found herself steering not toward the right-hand turn that would lead back to cut and soccer fields and polite married silence, but left— drawn by instinct more than decision. The Mason Hill Conference Suites came into view a few minutes later, tucked behind hedges and discreet signage. She pulled into the farthest corner of the parking lot, turned off the ignition, and sat in silence.

She hadn't planned to go there.

She hadn't planned to even think about it.

But the weight of it had been pressing against her chest all afternoon—the memory of that night, the key card, the envelope filled with thirty crisp $100 bills, and the blood. So much blood.

She stared up at the sixth floor and tried to picture it. Room 604.

One year ago, and still it lived inside her, like marrow.

After several minutes, she pulled away, her heart heavier but no clearer than before.

By the time Claire pulled into the driveway, the sky had turned a dusky mauve, the last of the sunlight slipping behind the trees in gauzy streaks. Her fingers were still tight around the steering wheel, her knuckles pale and aching, but she forced herself to loosen them, one by one, before killing the engine.

Through the front window, she could see the familiar glow of the television flickering against the living room wall. The shadows of her daughters flitted past—light, fast movements, a blur of limbs and hair and carefree noise.

She sat in the car a moment longer, inhaling deeply through her nose and holding it there, as if she could pressurize her nerves into something manageable. Something that wouldn't bleed through the cracks.

By the time Claire pulled into the driveway, the sky had turned a dusky mauve, the last of the sunlight slipping behind the trees in gauzy streaks. Her fingers were still tight around the steering wheel, her knuckles pale and aching, but she forced herself to loosen them, one by one, before killing the engine.

Through the front window, she could see the familiar flicker of the television glowing against the living room walls. A blur of movement passed in front of it—Emma or Sadie, she couldn't tell which—and then Mark appeared in the background, crossing the room with a snack bowl in hand.

She opened the door, stepped out into the thick evening air, and walked up the path slowly, steadying her breath. When she stepped inside, the scent of strawberry shampoo and buttery microwave popcorn wrapped around her like a domestic fog.

Sadie was curled up under a fuzzy pink blanket, her tablet glowing in her lap. Emma was splayed on the rug nearby, sketching in a notebook with one earbud dangling. Mark was reclined on the sectional, legs stretched out, feet bare, a bowl of pretzels balanced on his chest.

He looked up as the door shut behind her. "You were gone forever. What'd you get, the entire store?"

Claire set her purse on the counter. "I didn't buy anything."

Emma looked up. "Wait, no yogurt drinks?"

Claire blinked, trying to remember what it was they liked. She shook her head. "No. I just... wasn't feeling it."

Mark's brow furrowed. "You drove all the way there and came home empty-handed?"

"I needed air."

He sat up slightly. "You said you were picking up dinner."

"I changed my mind."

He gave a low, skeptical hum and stood, stretching with exaggerated slowness. "You always come back with something. Grapes, crackers, organic something-or-other."

"I didn't today."

His gaze lingered on her—longer than necessary, sharp enough to catch her off balance. "You're sure everything's okay?"

She forced a smile. "Of course."

Mark nodded once, but the weight of his silence pressed into her like a thumb on a bruise. He moved toward the sink and rinsed his hands, then leaned casually on the counter, studying her like a stranger.

"You've been quiet lately."

"I didn't realize that was a problem."

"It's not. Just... new."

Claire busied herself adjusting the vase on the table, a small shift for the sake of movement. "Everyone's allowed a bad week."

"Is this a bad week?"

She glanced up at him then, searching his face for meaning, but found only detachment. A casual curiosity that masked something colder. Calculating.

"I'm fine, Mark."

His eyes didn't leave hers. "You always say that."

She didn't reply. Couldn't. Her throat was tight, her heartbeat suddenly louder than the TV.

He turned, finally, and started toward the hallway. "We should take the girls to the lake house next weekend."

Claire hesitated. "I thought we agreed to go together next month."

He shrugged. "Actually I think maybe just me and the girls this time. Give you space."

She didn't respond. Because there it was again—him rewriting the plan, recasting himself as the benevolent father while quietly boxing her out.

He paused at the foot of the stairs. "Unless you'd rather we stay?"

She opened her mouth, then closed it. "Do whatever you want."

He smiled. "You're sure everything's okay?"

The words looped again. Louder this time.

She turned away, focusing on the forgotten vase again. "Perfectly."

When she finally exhaled, she was alone in the kitchen. The sounds of the television, the girls' laughter, Mark's footsteps upstairs—all of it muffled. Distant. Her hands trembled as she picked up the purse she'd just set down.

Because if Mark didn't know anything, he was just a cold, withholding man who no longer saw her. But if he *did* know—if he was planting these quiet landmines, waiting for her to crack—

Then he was playing a game she didn't understand.

And that might be even worse.

The girls were in their own rooms, tucked beneath blankets still warm from the dryer, their hair damp from quick evening baths and scented faintly like watermelon de-tangler and cherry bubble bath. Emma had chosen her usual perch— cross-legged in bed, earbuds in, sketchpad balanced on her knees. Sadie had demanded mac and cheese for dinner and was now curled up beneath her unicorn quilt, surrounded by an army of plush animals arranged with chaotic precision.

Claire moved between the two rooms in a practiced rhythm—checking windows, smoothing covers, dimming lights. A kiss on each forehead. A whispered goodnight.

By the time she stepped out into the hallway, the house had gone still.

Not peaceful. Still.

The kind of quiet that felt like it had weight behind it. Like something was pressing against the walls from the outside.

She lingered a moment longer outside Emma's door, listening to the soft scratch of pencil against paper, then turned toward her own room. She didn't want to go back downstairs. Not yet. Mark was probably still in the kitchen, replaying the day in his head, wondering what she hadn't said.

She crossed to the bedroom, phone in hand, thumb hovering over a familiar contact.

Meredith

Claire waited until the house settled. Until the last of Sadie's giggles faded, until Emma's door clicked softly shut, until Mark's shower stopped and the faint sound of him brushing his teeth echoed from behind their closed door. Then she slipped into the guest bathroom, quietly, barefoot, the burner phone still buried in the box, untouched again for now.

But her regular phone was in her hand. And her thumb hovered for only a moment before pressing the name she needed most.

Meredith.

It rang twice.

"Claire?" Meredith answered, her voice warm and sleepy, the kind of sleepy that sounded effortless and lovely and wrapped in lavender linen. "Everything okay?"   Claire hesitated. "Yeah. I just… needed to hear a friendly voice."

"Aww, honey." Meredith's voice immediately softened into the lull of concern. "You sound awful. What happened?" Claire sank into the edge of the couch, her throat suddenly tight. "I ran into someone today. At the store. I think he might've recognized me—from years ago, he seemed kind of creepy.."

There was the faintest pause. Not even a full second, but just long enough for Claire to notice it.

"Recognized you how?" Meredith asked lightly, carefully.

"Like… from when I lived in the city. Before Mark. He didn't look familiar, I'm just rattled that he knew me, it was unsettling, that's all."

Meredith made a little sympathetic sound, the kind Claire had come to depend on. "Oh no. Claire, people are weird. It was probably nothing. You're stunning — of course he thought he knew you," but something about the words felt rehearsed. Or maybe she was just being paranoid.

"Maybe."

There was a quiet rustle on the other end, the sound of fabric shifting — Meredith curling into bed, probably, hair loose, face clean, her world peaceful and untouched.

"You're safe now," Meredith said. "Whatever that man thought he saw, he didn't."

Claire closed her eyes. "Thank you."

"I mean it," Meredith whispered. "You're one of the good ones."

A pause.

And then, just before the call ended, Meredith added— softly, so softly that Claire almost didn't catch it:

"Besides, it's not like anyone really knows what happened... right?"

The words hung in the silence like smoke.

Claire blinked, lips parting.

"What?"

"Nothing," Meredith said quickly, her tone laced with a smile. "Just rambling. Go get some sleep. You sound like you need it."

Claire ended the call a minute later, still staring at the phone screen long after Meredith's name had disappeared.

She tried to shake it off. Tried to chalk it up to exhaustion.

But something inside her had shifted.

Just a fraction.

Claire ended the call and set the phone down beside her, still warm from the press of her hand. Meredith's voice, sweet and smooth as honey, lingered in her mind like a scent— familiar, comforting, just a little too well-timed. The question she'd whispered—so soft Claire had almost missed it—was still ringing in her ears.

Besides, it's not like anyone really knows what happened... right?

Claire stared ahead at the wall, silent, her expression blank. She didn't respond out loud. She didn't move for a full thirty seconds. Then, with practiced ease, she rose from the couch, smoothed the front of her sweater, and walked downstairs.

Mark was in the living room, the glow of his phone painting a faint blue sheen across his face. He didn't look up when she entered. Didn't say anything at first. He just scrolled, thumb sweeping in lazy repetition, jaw slightly clenched.

She stood there for a beat, arms folded. "Everything okay?"

He didn't flinch. "Fine."

She waited, but that was all he offered. No glance, no smile, not even a flicker of acknowledgment that she'd spoken.

Claire moved to the edge of the couch, keeping a polite distance. "Heading to bed," she said evenly.

Mark nodded without looking away from the screen. "Don't wait up."

She didn't ask where he'd be. Didn't ask why he'd said it like that—half-dismissive, half-daring. She knew the tone. It was the same one he used when he wanted her to press, to argue, to chase a truth he'd already tucked out of reach. She wouldn't give him the satisfaction.

"Night," she said instead, then turned and walked back down the hall to the bedroom.

The light in the ensuite bathroom was soft and golden. She closed the door behind her and leaned briefly against it, exhaling through her nose as she undid the top button of her blouse. It slid from her shoulders like an old skin. Her jeans followed, then the rest—each piece folded with the quiet efficiency of someone well-practiced at disappearing into themselves.

She reached into the top drawer of her vanity where she kept nightclothes and underwear, bypassing the stack of oversized tees and cotton lounge pants, and pulled out the silk pajamas she hadn't worn in months. They were cool against her skin, the champagne fabric whispering over her hips as she slipped the pants on, then eased into the top and fastened each delicate button.

She washed her face in slow, circular movements. Her reflection in the mirror looked calm, even serene. But there was a flicker in her eyes—something raw and sharp, like the glint of a blade just beneath the surface.

After brushing her teeth, she wiped down the counter— because habit demanded order—and turned off the light. In the bedroom, the sheets were pulled back, the pillows plumped. Mark hadn't come in. He wasn't coming. Not yet.

She flicked off the bathroom lights and moved to the bedroom window on her side of the king sized bed.

The blinds were still open. The moonlight spilled across the carpet in pale ribbons, soft and silvery. Claire reached for the cord, preparing to draw them closed—but then she paused.

Something outside caught her eye.

She stilled, hand hovering.

Across the street, just past the bend in the sidewalk, a dark car sat idle at the curb. No headlights. No movement. Just the shape of it, angular and quiet, nestled in shadow like it belonged there.

But it didn't.

Not on their street.

Not at this hour.

Claire squinted, stepping closer. The air in the room seemed to shift, thickening around her as she leaned slightly forward, just enough to get a better look.

There was someone in the driver's seat.

Barely visible.

But there.

A figure, motionless. Watching.

Claire's breath caught.

She didn't move. Didn't blink.

Her eyes adjusted slowly to the dark, parsing the figure from the shadows. She could just make out the line of a jaw, the pale shape of a face in the dark, tilted slightly upward.

Looking directly at her.

Her throat tightened. Every muscle in her body tensed, the way prey goes rigid in the presence of a predator. Not fear— something older. Something deeper. Like her instincts had beat her thoughts to the punch.

She stepped back from the window slowly, careful not to jostle the blinds, careful not to let the movement betray her.

Then, in one swift motion, she pulled the blinds closed.

The cord snapped gently against the window frame.

She stood there for a long moment, her back pressed to the wall, listening. To the house. To the silence.

Downstairs, a drawer opened. Mark? Possibly. But the timing was uncanny.

Claire reached for her phone again, fingers colder than before.

Whoever was in that car, they hadn't just stumbled onto her street. They weren't there for a drive, or a favor, or a GPS mistake.

They were watching.

They were waiting.

She slipped beneath the covers, heart pounding, every nerve screaming against the illusion of calm. The silk pajamas suddenly felt too soft, too vulnerable. Like armor made of air.

Outside, the wind stirred a low branch against the side of the house, a soft scraping sound like nails against glass.

She didn't sleep.

Not really.

Because now she knew—

The stranger in the store hadn't been random.

The matchbook wasn't the last warning.

And the past wasn't done with her.

Chapter Five

The Mask

Mark Holloway had always believed in order. That was the virtue, wasn't it? Structure. Rules. Predictability. These were the principles that underpinned a successful marriage, just as surely as beams held up the roof of a house. You followed the blueprint, you upheld the routine, and everything stayed intact. But if the seams began to fray — if the roof started to buckle — it wasn't because the design was flawed. It was because someone, somewhere, had stopped following the plan.

And lately, Claire had been improvising.

She thought he didn't notice. Thought she'd gotten better at slipping through the cracks of the day — inventing errands, disappearing mid-morning, returning with that carefully composed smile and hands conspicuously empty. But Mark noticed everything. The way her voice clipped slightly when she lied. The tight, distracted posture she wore like a second skin. The tremble in her fingers as she poured coffee without meeting his eyes.

He stood at the kitchen sink now, rinsing out his water bottle from his run, watching her across the room. She was at the pantry, robe cinched too neatly at the waist, hair twisted up like she was expecting to be seen — or caught. It was all a little too careful for someone who claimed she hadn't left the house. That's what she'd been lately: too careful. Always performing. Always on. And he hated how good she'd gotten at it.

Upstairs, the girls were still in pajamas, giggling through their second episode of cartoons. The sound drifted down like an echo of normalcy. Morning sunlight spilled across the hardwood in long, golden strips, dust motes catching in the air like suspended time. It was a stage set to look perfect — curated, sunlit, suburban. But beneath the veneer, Mark could smell it: the quiet rot of something unsaid.

And still, she kept up the act. Like he was too stupid to notice.

She didn't know he'd seen the burner phone. She didn't know he'd found it, hidden beneath a layer of expired coupons and dog-eared appliance manuals in the far corner of the kitchen drawer. That drawer was a graveyard for forgotten things — but this hadn't been forgotten. It had been hidden.

He hadn't powered it on. Didn't need to. A phone like that — cheap, anonymous, unsynced — had no business existing in a marriage built on fidelity and transparency. Unless it was carrying secrets. And Claire's secrets had begun to multiply.

But when he checked again the next morning, the drawer was clean. The burner phone was gone.

Moved.

She didn't even seem to realize he'd noticed. That silence said everything. It meant she was calculating. Strategic. She thought she was ahead.

Mark didn't confront her. He let the silence settle, dense and heavy, like humidity before a summer storm. Distance was a better weapon than anger. It coaxed more from her. Guilt made people overcorrect. And Claire had been overcorrecting for weeks now — smiling too brightly, asking too many casual questions, kissing him like a woman who wanted to be caught in the act of pretending everything was fine.

He watched her now with the cool detachment of someone assembling evidence. She pulled a box of cereal from the shelf, turned it over like she was actually reading the ingredients. Her hands were steady — too steady. Her face slack with the kind of calm that only came from rehearsal.

She thought she was fooling him.

He dried his hands slowly, letting the towel absorb more than water. Then crossed the room with deliberate slowness, mug in hand.

"You're up early," he said.

Claire turned slightly. "I've been up. The girls were hungry." He said nothing at first, letting the moment stretch like elastic. Then reached for the coffee pot and poured himself a cup, careful not to make eye contact.

"You know," he said finally, quiet but sharp, "you've been… distracted lately."

Claire blinked, her expression unreadable. "Have I?"

"Yes. And it's not just me who's noticed."

It wasn't true. No one had said a word. But that was the advantage of being married for over a decade. He knew exactly which lies worked best — the ones that left her unsure of how far the circle of suspicion had spread.

She didn't respond. Just stood there, one hand resting on the pantry door, as if waiting for her next cue.

The obedience of that gesture — the submission in her stillness — irritated him more than he expected. She looked like a woman who didn't know whether to fight or retreat.

And it occurred to him, with chilling clarity, that she had no idea who he was anymore.

"Who's noticed?" she asked, trying for lightness.

"Does it matter?"

"I think it does."

He took a slow sip of coffee, savoring the heat on his tongue.
"Let's just say people talk. You've been… inconsistent.

Guarded. Off."

She stepped away from the pantry, crossed the kitchen to the sink.

"Maybe I'm tired," she offered.

"You've been tired for months."

"I'm a mother."

He set the mug down with more force than necessary. "No," he said flatly. "You're hiding something."

Her hand hovered above the faucet, fingers curled slightly. Just the tiniest hesitation — but he saw it. That flicker. That stutter. The flaw in the performance. It was like watching the corner of a mask lift.

"I'm not hiding anything," Claire said, but the syllables dropped like pebbles in a deep, dark well — barely reaching the surface before vanishing.

Mark didn't answer at first. Just studied her. His eyes moved slowly over her features like a man memorizing the face of a liar, the face of someone he once knew. The silence thickened again, this time with heat — not the romantic kind, but the quiet burn of suspicion turned inward, of a man wondering how long he'd been made a fool of.

"If there's something I should know," he said, his voice low, "now's the time to say it."

She turned toward him. For once, her eyes met his directly. "Are you accusing me of something?"

He smiled. Thin. Brittle. "Should I be?"

That landed harder than it should have. Claire turned away slowly, as if distancing herself would restore equilibrium, or at least provide the illusion of it. He let her walk. That was always her move — retreat and regroup. But what she didn't realize was that the game had changed. He wasn't just watching now. He was hunting.

Mark remained where he was for a moment longer, fingers drumming absently against the marble counter. Then he glanced over at the small decorative clock above the stove. Just past nine. A good time. The girls would be preoccupied upstairs. Claire would be moving through her morning rituals. And he — he had work to do.

He retrieved his phone from the island and stepped into the hallway, out of sight. His fingers moved without thought, muscle memory guiding him to a private browser, a tucked away login, a forgotten account she'd never think to disable.

Her credentials still worked.

He exhaled through his nose, sharp and bitter, and stared at the location history. Her phone wasn't trackable now — either off or in airplane mode, another deliberate choice she probably thought he wouldn't notice. But the last ping… not the grocery store. Not Oakridge Elementary. Not even the park.

Mason Hill Conference Suites.

A hotel.

The name burned.

His jaw flexed, tension pulling tight at the hinge. He didn't slam the phone down. Didn't pace. Just stared at the tiny address on the screen until the text blurred. A hotel. And not even one with charm. Not some accidental stop. Not something she could explain away with an errand or excuse. It was deliberate.

She was lying.

And she was slipping.

He put the phone back in his pocket and walked with quiet precision through the house, like a man calculating a slow descent. This wasn't about anger anymore. It wasn't even about hurt. It was about control. And she was losing hers.

Later that day, after a shallow, forgettable lunch and an afternoon spent pretending to be occupied while Claire ferried the girls to their respective corners of the house — Sadie with her dolls, Emma with her sketchbook — Mark waited. Patience was everything. He waited until Claire took the girls upstairs for their evening routine. The rhythm of bath time was a perfect shield — running water, shrieking laughter, the thud of plastic toys against tile. He moved soundlessly through the downstairs, every step practiced, almost clinical.

He didn't go to her laptop first. Too obvious. No — he started with the drawer. The second drawer. The one she never opened when he was in the room. A month ago, she'd called it a "reorganization," clearing clutter, paring down. But Mark remembered that morning too clearly — she'd sat at the table unmoving for ten minutes straight, fingers locked around her coffee mug like she was bracing for impact.

Now, the drawer yielded nothing. Too neat. Too curated. No dust, no debris, not even a stray twist tie. No one lived this way — unless they had something to hide.

He moved next to her desk, crouched beside the slim trash bin, its contents stacked in careful layers. He rifled gently, methodically. A school craft. A grocery store flyer. Then beneath that, something more interesting: a torn envelope. Not just ripped — quartered and folded again. The kind of tear that comes from needing to erase something. The name on the front was slightly smudged, but not enough to be missed:

David

Mark didn't recognize it. But that didn't matter. The name itself was enough. She'd tried to destroy it — and in doing so, had left behind a footprint.

He stood, pulse ticking faster, and moved to the mudroom. Her purse hung in its usual place, lined up with military precision on the hook just below his own. Always zipped. Always immaculate. He hesitated only briefly before reaching for it.

The leather sighed as it opened.

Inside: lipstick, tissues, gum. Nothing. At first.

Then his fingers brushed a hidden zipper in the lining — one he'd never noticed before. And tucked within it, like a confession, were two objects that made the air in the room shift.

A matchbook. Black, matte. Logo embossed in silver serif: **Mason Hill Conference Suites.**

And a business card, slightly bent at the corner:

Detective Ray Hollis

Homicide Division

His number circled twice.

Mark didn't take anything. Didn't pocket them. Just stared — letting the image sink in. A matchbook and a homicide detective's card. Hidden in her purse. This wasn't distraction. This wasn't exhaustion or a midlife crisis or a hormonal imbalance. This was something else.

Something calculated.

Something dangerous.

He closed the purse quietly. And for the first time in their marriage, Mark felt the presence of something he hadn't been able to name before: fear.

That night, after the girls had fallen into sleep's syrupy lull and Claire had slipped into her room with the door shut— not locked, never locked, because locked meant guilt—Mark lingered in the den. The house was hushed but not peaceful. The silence held a charge now, like static clinging to the edges of a storm.

He didn't turn on any lights.

Instead, he moved to the fireplace, barefoot, the skin of his heels catching slightly on the wool rug as he stepped across the room. The hearth stood empty, sterile, flanked by decorative candle holders she dusted every Sunday like it mattered. The stack of mail on the console table had been sorted earlier—bills clipped, flyers trashed—but something had caught his eye. Not the content, but the envelope itself. The life insurance statement. It was still there.

He picked it up—not because he needed to, but because the weight of it was oddly satisfying. Tangible. Real. A contract for catastrophe.

He had taken out the policy seven years ago, in the hopeful haze after Sadie was born. He remembered sitting at the kitchen island with the paperwork spread in front of him, cradling a coffee Claire had made, feeling like a man stepping into responsible adulthood. Back then, the idea of Claire's death had been unthinkable. He couldn't even say it out loud. She was vibrant, young, ethereal in the way beautiful women sometimes are when life hasn't worn them down. Back then, she was the best thing about him.

Now, the pages felt cold. Clinical.

And when he flipped to the back, her handwriting still lived there in the margin—soft and feminine:
"Do we need this much coverage? Seems extreme."

It had made sense at the time. A beautiful wife, two kids, a mortgage, an image to protect. Now… it felt like something else. Like a thread he could pull if everything finally snapped. Like a release valve he wasn't supposed to touch.

Mark folded the statement again and let it slide back onto the stack. His gaze wandered to the glass-fronted cabinet beside the window seat. The one Claire kept pretending was too cluttered to organize, though he knew better. Inside were old photo albums, silver frames, things they hadn't displayed since moving into this house—tokens of a more hopeful era.

He opened the door, careful not to make a sound, and pulled free the heavy silver frame that had once sat on their first apartment mantle. Their wedding photo. Black and white. Shot in soft focus like a memory too tender to hold still. Claire looked luminous in it—timeless, almost. Hair pinned back, lips parted in a smile that wasn't for the camera but for him. A smile that once made him feel chosen.

He stared at it for a long time. His younger self looked back with unearned confidence, eyes too bright, too certain. The photo hadn't yellowed, but something inside him had.

He slid the picture from the frame with careful fingers. The thick photo paper bent but didn't break. He folded it once, then again, until Claire's smile disappeared into a sharp crease.

Then he dropped it into the fireplace.

And struck a match.

The flame took greedily. First the edges, then the dress. Her silhouette blurred, his own face dissolved. Smoke curled upward in slow ribbons, swallowing the past in silence.

When it was gone, he stood still, listening to the faint hiss of paper turning to ash.

He told himself he wasn't mourning anything.

The smell of smoke and ash lingered.

By the time he padded upstairs, the sharp sting of scorched paper still hung in the air—threading itself through the notes of vanilla Claire always left behind, like her signature. A scented candle, a linen spray, some soft-edged ritual she clung to. But tonight, the sugary warmth seemed cloying. A coverup. A disguise.

He moved silently past the girls' rooms—Emma's white noise machine humming like a heartbeat through the wall, Sadie's door cracked just wide enough for her stuffed fox to peek through. He paused, just briefly, at each threshold, letting the sight of their peaceful rooms soften something in him.

And then he reached the master bedroom.

The door creaked slightly as he opened it, and inside, the air was still and cold. Claire lay on her side, blankets pulled high, her form perfectly still beneath the sheets. Her back was to him, spine curved like a comma, hair tucked neatly behind one ear. A sleeping woman. Or the shape of one.

He stood there for a long moment, unmoving. Just watching her breathe.

There was something too posed about it all—too symmetrical. The blanket tucked exactly under her chin, the pillow slightly dented but not disheveled. Claire didn't sleep like that. Not unless she was trying to send a message.

Even in sleep, she curated herself into an instagram worthy picture of perfect slumber. Just like she curated their house, their life, their story. She didn't sleep like statue. Something was definitely up.

He didn't speak. He didn't undress. He simply climbed in beside her, turned off the light, and lay flat on his back with his eyes open to the dark.

And he thought of Meredith.

Not in a lascivious way—but with a clarity that made his breath slow. Meredith, who laughed easily and touched his arm without flinching. Meredith, with her riot of red curls and wine-colored lipstick and the way she said his name like it still meant something. She understood structure. She made things seem possible.

Maybe if things were different…

He didn't finish the thought.

He rolled onto his side and stared at the wall until sleep found him.

But Claire didn't sleep

Claire lay still until his breathing changed. Until the slight shift of weight beside her became steady, unaware. Then— soundlessly, effortlessly—she slipped from the bed.

The hallway creaked beneath her bare feet, but only once. She'd memorized the boards years ago, knew which ones to avoid and which would carry her safely. Downstairs, the house exhaled around her—quiet and cavernous, as though waiting for something to happen.

It wasn't insomnia that brought her out of bed. It was instinct. A thrum beneath her ribs. A whisper at the nape of her neck. That sense she had honed in hotel rooms and elevators and late-night parking lots. Something was wrong.

In the kitchen, the dim glow from the stove clock painted long shadows across the counter.

That's when she saw it.

The cup.

The cup was back!

She opened the cabinet where she had placed that set of cups, where she had left the remaining three. She had stored those cups behind the fondue set in the highest cabinet—the furthest one back. No one would have found them unless they were looking. Unless they *knew her.*

Where there used to be three cups, there were now only two. And the one sitting on the kitchen counter had a new blood red lipstick mark pasted on to its lip.

It was not casually left. This was deliberately placed. Again.

Claire moved toward it slowly, the pressure in her chest tightening with each step.

She didn't touch it. Not right away.

Because beside it, tucked like a calling card, was a matchbook.

Mason Hill Conference Suites.

Her breath caught. Her throat went tight.

She picked it up with numb fingers. It was pristine—unused. But inside, folded neatly between the matchsticks, was a the detectives card, with a message written in hard red block letters.

YOU DIDN'T STAY HIDDEN LONG.

The card slipped from her fingers, landing softly on the tile.

A matchbook. The cup. The message.

Someone had been here. Not just here in her house—but here in *her mind*. They had known exactly what to leave behind. What would unravel her.

She felt the cold rise through her feet and settle in her chest. This wasn't just a warning.

It was a promise.

Whoever this was, they weren't guessing. They knew exactly what they were doing.

Chapter Six

The Voice

Monday arrived wrapped in a brittle, gray stillness, the kind of chill-tinged quiet that settled over the windows like breath on cold glass—too soft to scrape away, too present to ignore. Claire Holloway stood at the kitchen sink, a dishtowel coiled in her hands, watching a gust of wind ruffle the garden beds where the hydrangeas bowed low beneath the weight of last night's storm. Their petals, pale and rain-swollen, clung stubbornly to their stems like women who had endured too much and dared not break.

Behind her, the house stirred to life with the polite clatter of breakfast routines—bowls chiming, spoons scraping, cartoons echoing faintly from the living room. Yet none of it touched her. It all existed at a strange, unreachable distance, like music leaking through a wall. The light in the kitchen felt too white. Sterile. The sort of light that showed everything—especially the things one didn't want to see. It pooled in corners and sharpened shadows. It made the countertops gleam too brightly, the floorboards reflect too

much. Everything around her looked slightly overexposed, as if the house itself had begun to recoil from her presence.

Claire hadn't slept. The night had stretched out like a question she couldn't answer, her thoughts scattered and jagged beneath the low hum of Mark's breathing. He'd slept soundly, of course—he always did—his presence beside her an unwanted anchor. She lay still most of the night, staring up at the ceiling as the shadows shifted overhead like silent spectators, waiting for her to crack. At some point, she'd counted the ceiling fan's rotations in the dark, watched the minute hand crawl from three to four to five, her body growing heavier with every hour, her mind spinning tighter into itself.

The girls were in the dining nook now. Emma sat perched on her knees at the island, fingers nimbly fishing marshmallows from her cereal, while Sadie recited spelling words under her breath, each one punctuated by a bite of toast. Mark leaned against the counter, coffee mug in one hand, his phone in the other, glancing up every now and then with the studied detachment of someone who thought parenting was a presence rather than a practice. Claire watched him carefully—too carefully—and was careful not to look like she was watching at all. His hair was still damp from the shower. His shirt, though neatly pressed, had one corner untucked. She noticed everything now—every thread out of place.

She knew how to keep the rhythm. The choreography of morning. She packed lunches. She zipped coats. She made sure every sock had a match and every backpack held the right folder. Her hands moved mechanically, her lips smiled on cue. It wasn't performance anymore. It was reflex. A muscle memory she couldn't unlearn. The mask had fused to the bone long ago.

When the front door finally closed behind them, the house exhaled. So did she.

For a long moment, Claire stood frozen at the foot of the stairs, one hand lightly grazing the polished banister. The silence settled again, this time heavier—denser. Without the girls' laughter or Mark's footsteps, the quiet rang almost sacred, as if the house itself was holding its breath. She could hear the faint tick of the thermostat. The far-off whir of the fridge. The kind of silence that felt *aware* of itself. She climbed slowly.

In the bedroom, she crossed to the closet without turning on a light, careful not to disturb the illusion of calm she'd managed to manufacture. Her fingers skimmed past dresses she hadn't worn in years—chiffon, wool, silk—until she reached the far end, where her oldest coats hung like cloaks hiding a secret. The air back here was cooler, undisturbed. It smelled faintly of cedar and something older, something sealed. Behind them, tucked between a cardboard storage cube and an old dry-cleaning bag, was the shoebox.

She pulled it out gently, her knuckles tight. The box wasn't locked, but it may as well have been sealed with blood. Her hands trembled with a kind of reverence. Not fear—no, not yet—but a knowing. The way a woman might tremble before opening a letter she already knows will ruin her.

Inside the shoebox, the items lay in quiet accusation. The teacups were nestled together gently in the corner, the smooth porcelain of one of them still bearing the red smear of lipstick like a scar that refused to fade. Beside it sat the room key card from the Mason Hill Hotel and Conference Center, its plastic surface scratched but intact, its weight still heavy with implication. Just looking at it triggered a muscle spasm in her jaw—memory trying to override muscle.

The burner phone lay face-down, inert and cold, like a body awaiting identification. Its screen was blank, but she swore it radiated something—an energy, a pull, a threat. A photograph, folded once down the center, revealed only Claire's back—her face turned away, obscured by shadows, but unmistakable to anyone who truly knew her. That slant of the shoulders. That precise, deliberate step. The wig and dark coat might've been camouflage, but her body still betrayed her.

The matchbook still carried the scent of mint and smoke, a tactile reminder of the night everything changed. She hadn't even opened it again—not since it arrived—because she knew what waited inside. A time stamp. A location. A threat pretending to be casual. And tucked between these fragile remnants of a life Claire had fought to bury, the cream colored card from Detective Ray Hollis seemed to pulse with latent threat. His name, printed in neat black letters, may as well have been chiseled into stone.

Together, they formed a kind of constellation—each star representing a moment she had tried to forget, now burning brighter because she'd buried them too long.

Claire sat on the edge of the bed, the box resting on her lap like a coffin. She didn't open it right away. She stared at it first, her reflection ghosting in the glossy surface of the phone, her heartbeat slowing until it felt unnatural, like she was forcing it into rhythm. Even the act of sitting upright felt rehearsed—like she was playing herself in someone else's memory of her.

The message—*Room 604. I know what you did.*—still etched itself behind her eyelids every time she blinked.

She hadn't touched the burner phone since powering it down the day before. Her fingers moved toward it now, hovering, then retreating, as though it might bite. Her breath hitched when her thumb grazed the edge. Static danced in the back of her throat. It didn't ring. It didn't vibrate. But somehow, it still throbbed with the ghost of a presence. As if the message were still arriving.

Next, she picked up the photo. Folded. Silent. Her face was turned, her identity protected by a trick of light, but she knew—someone had been close enough to capture that moment. Someone had followed her. Watched her. Stalked her down that hallway with a camera, knowing exactly what they needed. And knowing she would never be able to prove it wasn't her.

The photo trembled in her hand. Not from fear exactly. From fury. From the slow realization that the past wasn't creeping up behind her—it had already caught up and was now walking beside her.

After staring at the contents of the shoebox for a long time, she closed the lid, and resolved to protect her new life and her family no matter what it took.

She took the box of secrets back to the hiding spot in her closet, and took a deep breath.

Claire closed the closet door slowly, careful not to let it creak, as if the box buried behind the coats could somehow hear her retreat. Her breath labored under the pressure, she descended the stairs, past the now-empty kitchen, its morning chaos waiting for her to clean it up, as a metaphor for her life, and so she got to work scrubbing breakfast dishes and wiping down the granite counters until they gleamed. She scrubbed a little harder than necessary. The sponge squealed against the porcelain. Her wedding ring clinked against the sink.

She wasn't cleaning. She was erasing.

Outside, the wind had picked up. The sky overhead shimmered that strange, almost wintry silver-blue—too bright and too bleak all at once. The kind of sky that made shadows fall longer than they should, as though time itself were stretching.

Claire heard the low whir of the mail truck retreating down the street, the mechanical squeal of its brakes punctuating the quiet like a warning. She waited a beat, her ears tuned not just to the present, but to the possibility of what might be coming. Then, slipping on her flats, she stepped onto the porch, the air sharp with the scent of damp mulch and something more elusive—an unease she couldn't name.

At the end of the drive, nestled in its usual perch, stood the mailbox, innocuous and dumb. Claire cast a glance up and down the street—no dark car idling nearby, no dog-walking neighbor to wave at, no joggers on their usual loops. Just stillness. And in that stillness, a hollowness that felt almost expectant.

She padded down the path and retrieved the mail.

Back inside, she moved like someone trying to re-enter her body after a nightmare. Her kitchen was spotless again. Everything where it belonged. She filled the kettle, brewed a cup of jasmine tea, and stood with her hands curled around the mug as the steam kissed her face.

She was just beginning to relax—just beginning to believe, foolishly, that the storm had passed for the day—when the landline rang.

The sound sliced through the quiet like a serrated blade.

Claire froze. The phone—so outdated it was practically ornamental—sat in its cradle on the side counter, blinking.

She hesitated for a breath, then picked up.

"Hello?"

"Mrs. Holloway?" a woman's voice said. "This is Marianne from Oakridge Elementary. I'm just calling to confirm— your brother will be picking up Emma and Sadie today at noon, is that correct?"

Claire blinked. Her stomach dropped like a stone in water. "I'm sorry—what did you say?"

"The call came in earlier this morning. A woman identifying herself as you phoned the office and said your brother would be picking them up due to a family emergency."

"I don't have a brother," Claire said. The words emerged flat and automatic, her throat suddenly dry. "And I didn't call."

There was a beat of silence on the other end—polite, uncomfortable, but alert.

"I see," the woman said quietly. "I'll make sure that note is removed, and the girls will remain until regular dismissal."

Claire's fingers clutched the receiver as she hung it up, her knuckles gone white. Her breath was coming too fast now, like her lungs were staging a quiet rebellion. Her thoughts sprinted ahead of her body.

It wasn't a prank. It wasn't a clerical error.

It was personal.

It was intentional.

Someone wanted her daughters.

Someone wanted her.

She moved quickly, grabbing her keys and handbag, already heading for the door. Her chest ached with the weight of panic—but she pushed it down, locked it beneath the calm mask of motherhood. She would get to the school. She would get to her girls. She would figure out who was doing this.

She had just reached for the doorknob when the hallway light flickered—once, then again—before going dark.

A second later, every light in the house cut out at once.

Not with a pop or a surge, but with a strange, synchronized stillness, like someone had flipped the world off at the breaker.

Claire froze.

Then came the unmistakable crackle of static from the kitchen.

Her head turned slowly, like her body was no longer under her own command.

The small radio Mark kept on the counter for morning news—a clunky black battery-operated box—lit up with an eerie green pulse. No one had touched it. It hadn't been turned on in weeks.

And then, from the brittle static, a man's voice emerged— distorted, whispery, close enough to raise the hairs on the back of her neck.

"…Delia… I know you're there…"

Claire backed away, inch by inch, until her shoulder met the doorframe. Her whole body stiffened. Her spine locked into place. That name—*Delia*—was not a name anyone in her current life should know. It was a ghost. A cipher. A mask she had peeled off and buried.

And now it was back.

Her past wasn't chasing her anymore.

It was already inside the house.

Whatever game was being played, it had crossed into something new now—something intimate. This wasn't just about her past anymore.

Someone wanted to make her lose her grip on the present.

Her past was a living, breathing thing. And now it was inside the sanctuary she had made for her family.

Claire stood frozen in the doorway, her back pressed to the wood, as if the simple pressure could anchor her to something solid. The kitchen remained cloaked in a strange, electrical hush. Even the refrigerator seemed to have quieted. That single word—Delia—still lingered in the air like smoke, curling into the corners of the room long after the voice had dissolved into static.

It wasn't just the name.

It was the way it had been said.

Not with curiosity. Not with recognition. But with ownership.

She counted five slow breaths before she forced herself to move, her limbs stiff with disbelief. Step by step, she crept forward, feet barely making contact with the tile. The radio's LED light had already dimmed. It was silent now, inert. Like a taunt. She reached out and brushed the top of the plastic dial with her fingertips. It was cold. Innocent. Harmless. As though nothing had happened.

But something had.

And she knew that voice.

Even buried beneath the static, even warped by distance, she recognized the tone.

It made something deep in her flinch.

Claire backed away, her arms tightening around herself like she could cinch in her own fear, keep it from spilling across the floor. Her thoughts scrambled for logic—for a plausible explanation—but there was none. Someone had spoken to her through a device that should not have been on. Someone had known to use that name. Someone had invaded her home.

She had only one thought now. The girls.

She bolted.

Grabbing her coat from the hook and keys from the tray, she flew out the front door and into the cold. Her breath curled visibly in the air, sharp and fast. She slid into the driver's seat, fumbled with the ignition, and peeled out of the driveway with a squeal of tires that startled a neighbor's dog but didn't slow her down.

The roads were nearly empty. Just past rush hour. The world felt eerily normal—traffic lights blinking dutifully, brake lights glowing soft red in the distance, the mundane rhythm of a weekday unfolding as if everything weren't quietly unraveling beneath it.

Claire's fingers gripped the steering wheel hard enough to turn her knuckles bone-white. Her eyes flicked to the rearview mirror again and again, scanning for a tail, for headlights that followed too precisely, for shadows that didn't match.

Let the memories come, just for a moment. She'd learned not to let them stay long—just a flicker here and there, like headlights through fog.

The hotel rooms always smelled like citrus cleaner and old cologne. The men were all different but somehow always the same—entitled, restless, controlling. They wanted power, not connection. They wanted to pay to own something, even if only for an hour. They smiled too wide. Their hands lingered too long. Some were cruel in ways they didn't even recognize as cruelty.

She hadn't kept the money. Not most of it. She'd burned through it back then like she was trying to erase where it came from. Spa days for friends she didn't like. Shoes she never wore. One Christmas she bought Mark a watch worth more than their rent at the time, just to see if she could pass for someone else entirely.

But it had all come with a price.

And now that price was coming due.

Something had changed in within Claire as she drove to the school. Some interior switch had flipped. The line between her past and her present—so carefully constructed, so meticulously reinforced—had been crossed. Not metaphorically. Not emotionally.

Physically.

Someone had breached her home and worse, they'd threatened the safety of her daughters.

Delia no longer belonged in this life. It had been burned away, buried beneath motherhood, marriage, dinner parties, and volunteer drives.

But now it had clawed its way to the surface.

Claire knew she couldn't run again.

She had to stay.

And whoever had done this was about to find out just how dangerous she could be when backed into a corner.

Chapter Seven

The Window

The road bent sharply, the tires skimming the rain-glossed asphalt like skaters on black ice, and Claire gripped the steering wheel tighter, her knuckles white and bloodless. The sky above loomed low and colorless, bruised with morning haze, as if the day itself was holding its breath. Her eyes flicked between the windshield—wide and forward facing, the path she had to take—and the rearview mirror, that smaller, crueler window to everything she could never outrun. Her reflection flashed in it for a moment: pale, tense, a stranger in her own skin. Then gone again. Just the empty road behind her. But she knew better. Nothing was ever truly behind her—not the girl she used to be, not the hotel room where everything ended, not the man who bled on the carpet while she stood trembling in silence, and not the dirty past of who she used to be.

A red light halted her at the corner of Oak Hollow and Mercer, her breath ragged in the silence. The radio buzzed faintly with static—no music, no voices—just that soft, hissing nothing. Like someone was listening. Like someone had always been listening. The light turned green. She didn't hesitate.

The school came into view like a mirage—familiar brick framed by tidy hedges and a cheerful sign out front announcing *Field Day This Friday! Volunteers Needed!* It felt obscene, that normalcy. That anyone could post signup sheets or worry about juice boxes while someone out there was pretending to be her. Planning to take her daughters.

She pulled into the lot crookedly, not caring that her tires nudged the curb. The main office was just inside, past the flagpole and beneath the overhang that once sheltered Emma during a sudden spring rain. Claire had watched from the car that day, warm coffee in hand, amused as Emma shrieked and danced in the downpour.

Now her hands shook as she threw the gear into park.

Inside, the air smelled like pencils and floor wax—clean in the artificial, institutional way that spoke of routine and order. Too bright. Too quiet. The fluorescent lights hummed overhead, casting everything in a hard, sterile glow that made even the cheerful bulletin boards look like they were trying too hard. Claire stepped over the threshold, her heartbeat knocking like a fist in her throat.

The secretary looked up, startled, as if Claire's entrance had sucked all the air from the room.

"Mrs. Holloway?" she said, already halfway standing.

Claire didn't waste time. "Where are they?"

"They're safe," the woman said quickly. "Still in class, we didn't—of course we didn't release them—"

Her voice trembled, the professional polish cracking just enough to show the fear beneath. That was the worst part.

Not just the call. Not just the imitation of her voice. But the fact that the school—this haven—was scared, too.

"She said she was you," the secretary whispered. "And that their uncle would be picking them up. But when we asked for verification, she hung up."

"I don't have a brother," Claire said, breathless.

"We know. We know." The woman nodded too many times, her nervous hands fidgeting with a stack of permission slips. "We just—protocol is to alert the parent immediately, and—"

Claire turned away mid-sentence, her eyes drawn to the window across the hallway. Her throat tightened.

A dark car. Parked across the street. Tinted windows. No plates. No movement. No reason to be there. But she knew it was watching. She felt it. A stillness that was too deliberate. A presence disguised as absence.

The school, the children, the safety she had built like a fortress—none of it had been enough. Her past hadn't just caught up. It had stepped onto school grounds. And waved.

Back home, Claire locked the door behind her with a series of mechanical clicks. One. Two. Three. She turned the deadbolt like it was a prayer. A seal. A desperate act of control in a world that had just shown her how porous it really was.

She moved through the house room by room, checking locks, closing blinds, pressing her hand briefly to each windowpane as though she could sense something—or someone—on the other side. It wasn't fear exactly. Not anymore. Fear was too soft, too pliable. This was closer to rage. To knowing. To the bone-deep recognition that someone had gotten too close, too fast, and she hadn't seen it coming.

Whoever was behind this wasn't just trying to scare her. They wanted her off balance. Unmoored. Dragged backward into a life she had buried so carefully.

She wanted to call Meredith. She even reached for her phone. But something in her hand paused—some gut-deep signal, quiet but firm. She had too much to say and as close as Meredith was, she just couldn't tell her everything, she didn't want her best friend to see her in a different light, as a different person. One who has an entire second life and secret past.

A voicemail buzzed a few minutes later.

"This is Detective Ray Hollis, following up on our previous outreach. I'd appreciate a quick callback regarding a few lingering questions about David Holbrook."

She deleted it instantly.

But her chest stayed tight. The name had weight. It hung in the air like fog. Heavy, clinging. It seeped into the corners of the room and settled in her lungs.

She hadn't heard that name in months—not since the day she buried Delia.

Delia didn't exist anymore.

And yet… someone was trying to dig her up.

The sun set like a wound, bleeding light through the cracks in the blinds. The amber edges of the day fell across the floor in crooked strips, casting shadows that looked too much like fingerprints.

Claire didn't light any lamps. She didn't want to be seen.

Instead, she stood at the window and stared at her reflection. Her own face looked wrong. Blurry. Too tired. Too altered by secrets. She swore she saw motion. Just a flicker. Like someone was on the porch. A suggestion of shape in the fading light.

She peeled the curtain back. Slowly.

Nothing.

And yet her skin wouldn't stop crawling.

She sat on the floor that night after the girls had gone to bed, wrapping her arms around herself. Her back against the cold wood paneling of the hallway. Her knees pulled tight to her chest. The house creaked around her, the kind of old,

shifting noise she used to ignore—but now every groan of the floorboards felt like a footstep. Every rustle felt like breath. The shadows stretched longer than they should have, elongating with every blink, the silence thick enough to press against her ribs.

Her body trembled.

She didn't cry.

She was too tired to cry.

All she could think about was the price. The cost of pretending. The burden of being the good wife.

She had worn that title like a medal once, now it felt like a facade. A costume stitched from expectation and silence. And now, like all costumes, it was beginning to unravel at the seams. The threadbare edge of it pricked her skin, reminding her that no lie—no matter how carefully tailored—could hold forever.

Claire heard Sadie scream upstairs.

Her heart slammed into her chest as she ran—full speed, two stairs at a time—only to find Sadie sitting in bed, wide-eyed, the television glowing behind her.

"Mommy, the tv just went on," she said. "It turned to a scary show."

Claire held her close, heart thundering. "It's okay," she whispered. "You're okay."

It had happened again. This was no coincidence. It just could't be.

She tucked Sadie in again, checked the windows, and crept back down the stairs. Her hands lingered on their foreheads longer than usual. She memorized their warmth. Memorized the shape of safety while she still had it.

The house was dark and still. Mark was still at work, or at the gym, or somewhere else. The uncertainty of his location had become normal. It wasn't that she didn't care—it was that caring had lost its shape. It had thinned into something intangible, like fog dissipating under a streetlamp—there, then gone.

She knew she'd locked the house like Fort Knox. Nobody could come in from outside. She was sure of it.

But when she turned the corner to the main entrance of the house, the front door was slightly ajar.

Just a sliver.

Just wide enough for someone to slip through.

Slip out.

The hallway air shifted—cooler, unsettled. The stillness had been punctured. She felt it not with her ears but in the fine hairs on the back of her neck, which rose all at once.

Someone had been inside their home.

And they had left through the front door.

Chapter Eight
The Gloves

Claire once again couldn't sleep. She got so little sleep these days that she almost believed she was hallucinating everything that was happening, but the tangible evidence she kept in her closet told her this was real. Her waking hours were worse than her nightmares. The fear she felt constantly kept her mostly awake, her mind racing through the night.

At times she dozed in staccato bursts, nerves twitching her awake at the slightest creak or shift of the wind.

Even in her short, feverish dreams, she couldn't outrun the sound of her daughter's scream—or the silence that followed. She lay on her side in the dark, watching the faint outline of the closet door, the shoebox behind her coats like a sealed tomb for the life she thought she'd buried. But the dead never stayed dead, did they?

By five-thirty, she was out of bed and already dressed.

No makeup. No jewelry. Just jeans, a faded navy T-shirt, and the softest bra she owned, the kind that didn't pinch or demand attention. Clothes chosen not for style but for utility.

For war. She braided her hair back tight and flat. No perfume. No rings. It wasn't a costume today—it was armor.

She moved through the house with surgical efficiency—packing lunches, setting breakfast out for the girls before they came downstairs, checking locks again even though she knew they were sealed tight.

She didn't touch the front door. Didn't open the curtains. The air felt different this morning, like something had moved through it overnight. Someone still watching.

She returned upstairs once again , the closet beckoned. The shoebox. She knelt, opened the door, and checked it again. Lipstick cups. Burner phone. Matchbook. Surveillance photo. Detective's card. All still there. She closed the lid just as she heard the floorboard behind her creak.

"Looking for something?" Mark's voice was quiet. Too quiet.

Claire startled, then recovered—just barely. She turned, still crouched, and saw him standing at the doorway. He was already dressed, in his joggers and that smug gray quarter zip he wore too often. His arms were crossed, mouth neutral, eyes unreadable.

"Just rotating things out."

Mark stepped inside the room. Not close, but closer than she wanted. He didn't break eye contact.

"You've been… distracted," he said. "The girls notice. I notice."

She didn't answer right away. Her heart kicked like a trapped bird. The room felt smaller now—his frame blocking the only exit.

"I've had a lot on my mind," she replied, carefully. Not defensive. Not too open.

He tilted his head, studying her like she was a stranger. Or worse—a liar he was trying to trap. "Anything you want to tell me?"

Her spine straightened. She had been a good wife. Better than he'd deserved.

She was the one who made sure the bills were paid on time, the birthdays remembered, the girls emotionally intact despite the distance in their home.

She cooked, cleaned, covered his laziness with perfectly curated smiles. She hadn't wanted anything from him except love. Real love. And even that, she'd stopped asking for.

She cleared her throat. "I don't think now's the time for this, Mark."

"When is?" His voice dropped half a step. Low. Controlled.

Claire's pulse climbed. She crossed her arms too now, mirroring him. "What exactly are you implying?"

Mark walked to the edge of the bed and sat down slowly, eyes still fixed on her. "You tell me."

The pause stretched between them like a live wire. Claire felt the heat rise in her chest. All the silent labor. The invisible sacrifices. How many nights had she laid next to him, pretending his coldness didn't freeze her to the bone?

How many mornings had she smiled for the girls while fighting to keep herself from vanishing?

She shook her head, voice trembling—but not from fear anymore. "You don't get to play the concerned husband now. Not after all this time."

"Claire," he said softly, but she heard it—that edge of condescension. The tone men used when they thought they were the only rational ones in the room.

And something in her snapped, quietly.

"I was the good wife," she whispered. "The best wife. And you didn't even see it."

Mark blinked.

She stepped toward him, just one step. "You never noticed the thousand ways I tried to hold this family together. The effort. The lies I told just to keep everything smooth. Do you even see me, Mark? Or just the reflection you want me to cast?"

His lips parted slightly, but he said nothing.

Claire exhaled, the rage cooling into something colder. Finer.
Like glass being shaped in a flame.

From the floor, a beam of early sunlight hit the corner of the closet door. It glinted off the brass handle like a wink. Claire didn't flinch. She was done hiding in shadows.

The morning unfolded with the usual routine, and Claire felt like she was moving around with the combination of a fire lit within, and a heavy rock of anxiety lodged in her sternum.

Mark grabbed his keys and ushered the girls out the door as Claire hastily kissed each daughter on the head as they left.

The door clicked shut behind them, and Claire stood frozen in the entryway, one hand still wrapped around the edge of the wall like she needed it to stay upright. The house exhaled into silence. No cartoons, no shoes squeaking against hardwood, no clipped voice commenting on traffic. Just her breath and the low, ambient hum of a life trying not to unravel.

She waited another moment to make sure they were truly gone—waited until she heard the car pull away and disappear down the street—before moving. And when she did, it was with purpose.

She moved through the kitchen like someone stepping onto a stage. Not aimless now. Not afraid.

She retrieved a small spiral-bound notebook from the drawer near the junk basket—one she used once for grocery lists— and flipped past the old pages of meal planning and coupons to the first blank sheet.

At the top, in small, blocky letters, she wrote:

TIMELINE:

Thursday - Cup, text message

Friday - Key card. Who's in that dark car?

Saturday - Photo with message on the back, visit from detective, stranger at the store (knew my name/s)

Sunday morning - (2am - cup is back, matchbook and note. Someone took it from my purse.) M?

Monday - Radio static voice.Someone tried to take Emma and Sadie, locked up house, someone was inside. Who???

Tuesday - 8:12 AM — Mark left with girls. House secure. No signs of forced entry. Call detective Hollis? Or wait?

Her handwriting was steadier than she expected. She paused, then wrote another line beneath it in hard, angry, determined block letters, she underlined it three times:

I WILL NOT BE HUNTED.

She sat down at the kitchen island, the same place where she used to fill out permission slips and birthday RSVPs, and opened the battered old Lenovo from the garage shelf. It wasn't hers. Not really. Not Claire Holloway's, anyway. This one belonged to Delia—the name she'd used back then.

She had kept the machine powered down for over a year, battery removed, wrapped in layers of ziplock and stuffed in a paint can behind the tool chest.

Now, on Wednesday morning, she booted it up. The fan whirred like it hadn't drawn breath in a decade. Claire entered the old password—d3lia.k123r—and watched the encrypted dashboard load.

She opened the private browser and navigated to the email service she used under Delia's name.

The name had been chosen at random once—a bottle of red wine, a French film on Netflix, a fleeting decision that somehow stuck. Jeff had liked it. Said it had a clean sound, high-class but untraceable. Jeff, the voice in the dark.

The man who arranged everything but never showed his face.

As she looked through her emails from her previous life, there were many from her handler, Jeff - who she had never met in person, but who put her in contact with her wealthy clients.

He booked the rooms under a fake name that couldn't be traced back to himself nor his girls, and he took a 30% cut from all of her earnings. She was instructed to leave the money in a lockbox in town, not far from her clean suburban home. She never met Jeff, but Jeff knew what she looked like, and he knew her real identity.

When she left the business a year ago, he told her that it was a clean cut, she could leave and he would never contact her again…but now, had he?

Claire clicked on the last email from Jeff, sent almost a year ago. It was brief and to the point, like all of Jeff's messages.

Her eyes scanned the lines: a reminder for her to stay cautious, and a promise of no kore contact. At the bottom, as always, he'd signed off with his trademark phrase:

"Go well, Missy."

She had never understood why he chose those words—half caring, half cryptic—but by now she was used to seeing that sign-off in every email and hearing it at the end of each voicemail he left on her burner phone. It was just his way of saying goodbye.

She exhaled and sat back, drumming her fingers anxiously on the desk. Jeff's message gave no new insight. The uncertainty gnawed at her.

Claire glanced at the silent burner phone lying next to the laptop—no new voicemails, no missed calls.

For all her communication with "Invisible Jeff," as she sometimes called him, he remained frustratingly elusive.

In moments like this, with nothing left to do but wait, she felt completely alone.

Suddenly, the quiet of her living room shattered with the sharp ring of her personal cell phone. Claire jolted, a spike of adrenaline shooting through her.

She snatched up the phone from the coffee table, nearly dropping it in her haste. An unsaved number flashed on the screen, but she recognized the area code and the last four digits — Detective Hollis had given her his number on a card when he visited. Why would he be calling now?

She took a steadying breath and answered, "Hello?" trying to keep her voice level.

"Ms. Holloway? This is Detective Hollis," came a measured, familiar voice.

His tone was warm and professional, the same reassuring cadence he'd used when he spoke to her at the house on Saturday.

Claire's taut shoulders eased a fraction. "Good evening, Detective," she said quietly. "Is everything alright?"

"I'm just checking in," Hollis replied. There was a gentle concern in his voice that almost put her at ease. "I wanted to know if your memory has jogged at all since we last spoke." "I am afraid I am as confused as you are, I do not know the deceased. I have never met him."

"Okay, I understand," he said kindly. "We haven't turned up any new leads on the situation yet, but we're keeping an eye on things. You have my number, so if you remember anything—anything at all—or if you notice anything out of the ordinary, you call me immediately. Alright?"

"I will," she assured him. "Thank you, Detective."

There was a brief pause on the line; a soft crackle of static filled the silence.

Hollis seemed to inhale as if steeling himself to say something more. "Alright then, Claire," he said slowly, almost fatherly. "You take care now, and…."

His voice shifted—just a subtle drop into a lower, more personal register.

The next words came out softly, almost lost in

the background hiss: "Go well, Missy." Claire's

blood turned to ice.

What did he just say?

For a split second, she wondered if she'd imagined it. But the call had already ended with a quiet click, leaving her staring at the glowing screen of her phone in stunned silence.

Her mind grappled with the two syllables that echoed in her ear, Missy, Missy, Missy, like a ghostly refrain.

Nobody called her "Missy." Nobody except Jeff.

Heart pounding, Claire slowly set the phone down.

Those words coming from Detective Hollis's mouth felt jarringly out of place. He'd been so formal with her, so careful and polite in all their interactions. Why would he use that phrase? It was almost… intimate. Familiar.

Her thoughts raced, trying to make sense of it, and then a memory bubbled up to the surface.

Detective Hollis had said those exact words once before. It was on Saturday, when he came by to talk to her. She had been anxious and distracted as he finished questioning her. He'd adjusted his hat, given her a polite smile at the door and, in parting, he said, "Go well, Missy," before walking away to his car. At the time, Claire had barely registered the odd farewell. It struck her as a quaint, old-fashioned phrase—a little quirky, but nothing noteworthy amidst the stress of having a detective at her door.

Now it hit her like a bolt of lightning.

Claire pressed a hand over her mouth as another memory flashed into crystal clarity. The stranger at the grocery store.

The man at the grocery store had said her name like it tasted familiar. That strange grin. The way he blocked her cart.

Now, in the silence of her kitchen, it clicked—something in his voice. Something she'd only ever heard over burner phone calls and encrypted voicemail drops.

He stood in produce aisle, in an oversized sports jacket and thick glasses who had said he knew her.

She remembered him—unremarkable, friendly smile, a baseball cap pulled low.

He'd chatted for only a minute. As he turned to leave, he tipped his cap and gave a peculiar little salute. And he said it. "Go well, Missy," in the same kindly tone. She had nearly laughed at the quaint expression; it was such an unusual way to say goodbye to a stranger. She'd dismissed it at once, assuming it was just his folksy mannerisms. But it was not a coincidence. It couldn't be.

Her fingers began to tremble as the puzzle pieces clicked together. Three different people—a mysterious handler named Jeff, a harmless stranger at the store, and a seasoned police detective—had all told her "Go well, Missy."

The exact same words, the exact same phrasing. Claire's breaths grew shallow. It was as if a veil was lifting from her eyes. They were not three people at all.

They were one and the same.

"Oh my God…" she whispered, the realization chilling her to the bone. Jeff.

It had always been Jeff. Her invisible handler, the man she knew only through encrypted emails and distorted voicemails, had been standing right in front of her more than once. Disguised as a stranger in the grocery store. Disguised as Detective Hollis, the officer she thought was protecting her.

A wave of dizziness washed over her as the room seemed to tilt.

Jeff had never been truly invisible—he had been here the whole time, wearing different faces like masks. He hadn't just been watching from a distance; he had infiltrated her life. He was the one in the dark car that she'd spotted idling at the end of the street. He was the one who had crept into her house when she wasn't home, proven by the subtle hints of disturbance only she would notice.

Claire's skin crawled at the thought of it. Jeff had orchestrated everything, moving her around like a chess piece, all while pretending to be a guardian angel on the phone and an ally in person.

The betrayal cut deeper than anything she'd ever felt.

Her shock soon mixed with anger and fear as her thoughts churned. Jeff couldn't have pulled this off alone... could he? He'd been a step ahead of her at every turn, somehow always knowing where she'd be, what she was planning. A gnawing suspicion coiled in her gut. Mark. Mark had access to her life in ways few others did. She remembered how Mark had acted oddly distant these past few days, how his eyes had flickered with something like guilt when she mentioned feeling watched. Was it possible he had been working with Jeff from the start?

Claire's jaw clenched. It was entirely possible that Mark had been the inside man—providing Jeff with her schedule, her vulnerabilities, maybe even a key to her house. That would explain how Jeff got in so easily. The thought made her stomach lurch. Someone she trusted might have betrayed her, too.

Claire realized she was clutching the edge of the counter so hard her knuckles had turned white. She forced herself to

breathe, to think. Her world had tilted on its axis in the span of a single phone call.

The detective she'd cautiously begun to trust was a lie. The creepy stranger in the store was a lie. Even Jeff's comforting distance was a lie—he'd been physically here, closer than she ever imagined, watching her under various disguises.

She didn't know what frightened her more: the fact that Jeff had managed to deceive her so completely, or the fact that he had easy access to her home and life.

Claire's eyes darted to the front window, half-expecting to see the silhouette of a man in a hat watching from across the street. The curtains stirred slightly in the night breeze, but she saw no one out there—nothing beyond the glass.

A cold, hard resolve began to form in the pit of her stomach, cutting through the fear. Jeff had been one step ahead of her at every turn, but now she knew.

She knew his secret. And that knowledge was power. Claire swallowed, her throat dry, and gently closed the laptop with Jeff's email still on the screen.

"Go well, Missy," he'd always said. As if he truly cared. As if it wasn't all part of some twisted game.

Claire pushed back from the desk and stood on unsteady legs. Enough. She wasn't going to be a pawn in his game any longer. Whoever Jeff really was—Detective Hollis, a random stranger - he had exposed himself with that one slip. Maybe he was even working with someone closer than she could have imagined - her own husband.

Upstairs, Claire stepped into her closet and knelt before the shoebox that held the artifacts of her nightmare. Inside were the tokens of this twisted game, all the evidence of how her old life had bled into her new one.

Her hand hesitated over the shoebox, then moved past it to a wicker basket tucked in the corner.

Neatly folded inside were remnants of Delia, the woman she used to become on dark nights: a set of lacy lingerie, black thigh-high stockings, and a pair of black satin, elbow-length gloves.

She used to wear those gloves with a slinky designer dress and red stiletto heels. The ensemble transformed her into someone polished, high-class.

In her past, the satin gloves gave her an air of elegance and control, a seductive armor that helped her play the role flawlessly.

Now, the gloves would serve a very different purpose. Claire's fingers trembled only slightly as she slid them on, one after the other, the cool silk molding to her skin. These weren't an accessory now—they were armor.

The delicate fabric hugged her arms up to the elbows, a stark contrast to the jeans and t-shirt she wore like battle fatigues. She flexed her hands, feeling the smooth material stretch over knuckles that ached for a fight.

In the faint light of the closet, Claire clenched her fists and stood up straighter. The woman who once used these gloves to allure and distract was gone. In her place stood a warrior donning satin gauntlets.

The gloves were on, and Claire was ready. Now it was her turn to act.

But first, she had to get out of this house. A prickling feeling on the back of her neck told her that if Jeff had gone this far, he could be watching her even now. She wouldn't be a sitting target. Grabbing her coat and the car keys, she made for the door.

As she stepped onto the walkway, one question pounded in her mind above all the others: How long had "Jeff" been this close to her?

The chilling answer , she feared, was from the very beginning. And if Mark was indeed helping him… well, then there was truly no one she could trust.

She couldn't be sure who anyone was. Her first thought was to tell Meredith everything, maybe she would be the only person who would have her back.

Locking the door behind her, Claire slipped into her car and started the engine. Her eyes flicked to the rear-view mirror.

In her imagination she almost expected to see Detective Hollis's piercing gaze or that stranger's friendly grin lurking in the back seat. Nothing. Only her own wide-eyed reflection stared back.

"No more," she whispered to herself, voice hardening as she pulled out of the driveway. Whether Jeff was in a patrol car or a dark SUV or hiding behind another identity altogether, Claire was done being prey.

The revelation of his parting words had turned her fear into determination. She didn't know exactly what she would do next—who she could turn to or where she could go—but one thing was certain.

She finally knew the truth. Jeff was here, in her world, under whatever mask he fancied. And now that she knew, the real game between them had begun.

Chapter Nine

The Room

The Mason Hill Suites hadn't changed.

That same lacquered awning still jutted out like a forced smile, the gold-trimmed doors glinting in the morning light with a kind of hollow, desperate cheer. It was the kind of place that pretended to be tasteful but reeked of quiet transgressions—where polished men with ruined hearts came to unfasten their lies in private.

Claire didn't dare park out front. She left her car two blocks down, walked the long edge of the property with her hood up, and stood across the street, watching. The building loomed, smug and silent.

A year had passed since Room 604, but the memory clung to her skin like damp air—too close, too knowing. Even from here, she felt it watching her. The hallway's stillness. The way the elevator had stalled for just one beat too long. The icy certainty that she had not been alone.

She hadn't planned to come here. Not consciously. Now she stood frozen on the sidewalk, pulse ticking high in her throat, staring at the sixth-floor window. She couldn't see it, not really—just a sliver of curtain drawn tight against the sun—but she knew. Room 604. Her graveyard. Her reckoning. The place where Delia had died, and Claire had been born again, forged in secrecy and shame.

The memories clawed their way to the surface, uninvited. She didn't need to see the room. She could still feel it. Smell it. The citrusy bite of overused disinfectant. The sickly cologne David wore. The panic in her throat when he grabbed her wrist that final time.

David Holbrook had liked power, not sex. He liked watching a woman undress while he stayed fully clothed. Liked to make her say thank you after every request. Liked to remind her that money meant ownership.

That night, she'd worn a black sheath dress, red heels, no jewelry—he liked things simple, stark. He'd pressed her against the wall when she flinched at his touch. Called her a whore. Told her she was nothing more than a high-end trick in lipstick. She'd pulled away, jaw locked. But when he shoved her—hard—against the dresser, she'd seen something flash in his eyes. Not just rage. Something more. Something broken. And that's when she left the room. Not out of fear. Out of necessity. To breathe. To survive. To take a call.

When she came back, he was on the floor, his head bleeding, gasping like a man who'd already seen what was coming for him. She never saw who else had entered. But someone had. Someone who didn't leave him breathing.
She hadn't answered her phone out of carelessness. The call came in just after David's outburst, just as her heels tapped toward the door and his voice sliced after her like a whip.

135

She stepped into the hallway, shut the door behind her, and slipped the phone from her clutch with trembling fingers. Unknown number. But she knew who it was.

The voice on the other end was low, calm, unhurried. They never said names. Never said much at all. Just a few clipped words: "Status?"

Claire's reply had been automatic, her training kicking in like muscle memory.

"Engaged. Unstable. Aborting."

A pause. Then: "Understood. Exit clean. No trace."

The call ended. She turned back toward the room. And in that small window of silence—between the command and her compliance—someone else had slipped inside.

She turned to the dresser where the payment lay waiting. It wasn't about the cash—never had been—but the envelope had been sitting there on the dresser like an accusation. Three thousand dollars, beside the glass he'd poured too full and the tie he'd loosened like he owned the air in the room. She'd hesitated for one second, maybe less. Then her hand closed around it like instinct. She hadn't even looked back. The last thing she heard was the faint rattle of his breath.

But in hindsight, the deeper violation had come earlier— weeks before, maybe even months—because somehow he had known her real name. Her real address. Claire Holloway. He wasn't supposed to know that. No one was. She hadn't told him, she hadn't slipped. But there'd been that one afternoon —just one—when she'd stepped into the bathroom and left her purse unzipped. She hadn't thought much of it at the time. Now, it made her stomach churn. He must've gone through it. Quietly. Carefully. Looking for something to use.   And then he used it.

The memory of that night clung to her like smoke. She wanted to wash it away. When Claire stepped through the front door, she didn't pause to drop her keys or take off her shoes. She moved with singular purpose, her limbs tight with tension, the breath in her lungs shallow and sour.

The house felt colder than it should have, its silence pressing inward like a held breath. She made a beeline for the shower, as though the steam might scald away the imprint of memory.

Under the punishing heat, she scrubbed hard at her skin, nails dragging across her arms as if she could peel away what clung to her—not dirt, but something darker. Guilt. History. The aftershocks of a past that had slithered, uninvited, into her present. Her hair clung to her back in wet strands. The water hit her collarbone in steady bursts. Still, she didn't move. Not until the water ran lukewarm and the room filled with mist thick enough to blur the mirror—and maybe, if she was lucky, her reflection with it.

Wrapped in a soft cardigan-style dress and a pair of worn lounge pants, she padded barefoot into the kitchen. The familiar rhythm of filling the kettle, lighting the burner, reaching for the chamomile tin—it was muscle memory, not comfort. A ritual of pretending things were normal.

She sat at the counter, hands wrapped loosely around a mug she hadn't yet poured, her fingers twitching from the inside out. What she wanted was simple, and impossibly complex: someone to talk to. Someone who might understand, without needing the whole truth spelled out.

She pressed her palms flat against the cool granite, stared at the silent kettle, and listened to the ticking of the kitchen clock.

She'd always known that Mark was incapable of gentleness for very long. Even in their best seasons—their golden weeks after moving to the new house, when the girls were still small and every night ended with white wine on the porch—there had been a tightness to him. A defensiveness. She used to think it was just stress, the strain of work, the exhaustion of new parenthood. But now she was beginning to wonder if that brittle edge had always been something else. Something darker.

Mark hadn't asked her about the call from the school. He hadn't asked her why she flinched when the phone rang or why she checked the locks three times before bed. But he had started coming home earlier, picking at her reactions like he was looking for a tell. And the way he watched her when she reached for her purse or checked her messages—it wasn't protectiveness. It was assessment. Like he was measuring her silence, trying to find the crack.

She didn't trust him. Not anymore. Not entirely.

And the worst part was, she couldn't tell if that feeling came from her own guilt or if it was a warning.

Claire scrolled slowly through her contacts, thumb hovering over Meredith's name. Her finger tapped almost on reflex, before she could talk herself out of it.

"Hey, you," Meredith answered cheerily, her voice like chamomile tea and warm bread—safe, familiar. "How are the girls?"

"They're fine," Claire said, her voice already strained.

But she wasn't calling to talk about the girls.

There was a pause on the other end. Meredith knew. She always seemed to know when something wasn't right. "What's wrong?"
Claire hesitated. Then, in the softest whisper, "It's Mark."

A beat. "Did he… Claire, did he do something?"

"No," Claire said quickly. Too quickly. "Not really. He's just… I don't know how to explain it. He's different lately. Cold. Like he's angry with me all the time but won't say why."

"Has he said anything?" Meredith asked, cautious now. "Anything that makes you feel unsafe?"

Claire looked out the window, watching the movement of the trees, the shimmer of sunlight on the glass. "He just… watches me. Like he's waiting for something. And I keep thinking—what if I'm not imagining it? What if there is something?"

"You're scaring me," Meredith said. "You know you can tell me anything, right?"

Claire swallowed. Her throat felt tight, brittle.
"I don't know who I can trust right now."

Another pause.

Meredith's voice softened. "Then start with me."

Claire's breath hitched. She wanted to tell her everything—what she was in her past life, what happened a year ago in Room 604, how she hid herself afterward, and what she's going through now. But she couldn't. Meredith didn't know about Delia. She didn't know about David or Room 604 or the envelope full of cash that still sat, like guilt made manifest, inside Claire's closet.

"I just needed to talk," Claire said. "That's all."

"Anytime. You know that."

They hung up, and Claire set the phone down on the counter like it had burned her.
Even with Meredith's voice still ringing in her ear, she'd never felt more alone.

Chapter Ten

The Friend

Meredith exhaled slowly through her nose, steadying her breath the way she used to before stepping on stage. Not that she performed anymore. But her body still remembered the ritual—how to slow the pulse, lift the chin, soften the gaze. Calm was a practiced thing. It didn't always come naturally, but with enough repetition, it could look effortless. Even now, so many years later, the same tools still served her. Breath. Posture. Stillness.

In another life, she'd stood in front of grand pianos and low lighting, a vintage mic cradled in one gloved hand, smoke curling in the corners of dark rooms like a secret no one dared to name. Her voice had been velvet, deliberate. She never rushed a lyric. Never filled a silence that hadn't earned breaking. There was an intimacy in that restraint. A power.

Men and women alike used to stop mid-sip to watch her sing. They'd lean in as if her voice could grant them something—permission, absolution, seduction. And in a way, it had. She had understood power then. Understood its elegance, its weightless precision. To command a room with softness—that was mastery. That was art.

The cashmere robe clung lightly to her shoulders as she moved through the bedroom, its hem whispering across her thighs with each step. The fabric was the color of pale ash, a quiet luxury. Her bare feet padded silent against the wood, her steps unhurried, reverent, like she was walking through a cathedral built of control. She never rushed in her own space. Time bent here, willingly. A single wine glass rested on the nightstand, still half full, rim smudged faintly with lipstick the color of dried rose petals. Her shade. Her signature.

Outside, the hedges stood clipped into obedient shapes. The gardener came on Tuesdays, whether she was home or not. She liked that. Order without effort. Structure without consequence. Clean edges in a world where so few things stayed in their proper place.

She passed the mirror without glancing at it. Not because she feared what she'd see, but because she already knew. She sat at the edge of her bed instead, the mattress barely dipping beneath her. Hands folded in her lap. Eyes unfocused, fixed on nothing but the softness of the morning light curling along the far wall. The silence wasn't lonely. It was curated. Intentional. A stillness she had designed for herself after dismantling a life that no longer served her.

She had built her life deliberately, like a sculpture—shaping it until it held exactly what she wanted and no more. Wealth came from a portfolio she managed herself. Elegance, from knowing restraint. Privacy, from never letting anyone see her when she wasn't composed. She had banished chaos from her world like an infection. Now, everything she touched gleamed. Her home, her routines, even her grief—they all shimmered with purpose.

At thirty-six, she'd ended a marriage. It had nearly undone her. Not because she missed him—no, not him—but because of what she had lost along with the illusion. She didn't talk about it. When people asked, she smiled sadly, and said, "It's too painful to talk about." They always nodded. It was enough. No one questioned a woman who looked that graceful in her grief. It was the perfect armor. Tragedy, tastefully worn.

The phone buzzed once on the side table, its vibration a soft pulse against the lacquered wood.

Claire.

Meredith picked it up, thumb brushing the screen, voice already wrapped in velvet by the time she answered. A practiced purr.

"Hey, you."

A breath on the other end. Then Claire, sounding like she'd run miles without moving.
"Hi." She murmured. Just one word, but Meredith felt the fracture in it.
"How are the girls?" Meredith asked sweetly, her tone light, as if nothing were wrong. As if the air hadn't already thickened. As if she didn't already know the call wasn't casual.

"They're fine." Came Claire's strained voice. A tightness there. Meredith could hear it—the careful pressure of a woman holding her world together with thread.

She knew Claire wasn't calling to talk about the girls.

"What's wrong?" she asked, not pressing, not too gentle either—just enough concern to sound sincere.
A hesitation, taut and full of dread.

Then, in the softest whisper: "It's Mark."

Meredith's voice dropped an octave. "Did he… Claire, did he do something?"

"No," Claire said quickly. Too quickly. "Not really. He's just… I don't know how to explain it. He's different lately. Cold. Like he's angry with me all the time but won't say why."

Meredith straightened slightly, spine lengthening like a reed in water. "Has he said anything?" she asked, cautious now. "Anything that makes you feel unsafe?"

Claire's silence lingered just a second too long. Then: "He just… watches me. Like he's waiting for something. And I keep thinking—what if I'm not imagining it? What if there is something?"

"You're scaring me," Meredith said softly. "You know you can tell me anything, right?"

"I don't know who I can trust right now."

Another pause. A breath passed between them, thick as fog. Meredith's voice softened like silk folding at the seam. "Then start with me."

"I just needed to talk," Claire said. "That's all."

"Anytime. You know that." Replied Meredith.

When the call ended, Meredith didn't move for a long time. The phone rested in her hand, screen gone black. Her reflection hovered faintly in the glass—lips slightly parted, eyes steady. She studied her own silhouette in the dim surface, the sharp outline of her jaw, the stillness in her expression. The calm that had taken years to perfect.

She rose without a word, fluid and feline, and crossed the floor with the quiet grace of someone who owned every inch of her surroundings. In the kitchen, she poured another glass of wine, this one fuller than the last. The bottle gave a soft glug as the liquid rose in the crystal, a muted sound that echoed in the stillness like a blessing.

The silence wrapped around her again—not as comfort, but as confirmation. She didn't need anyone to fill the silence. It served her better empty. Silence gave her control. Noise invited error.

As she passed the mirror on her way out, she allowed herself a single glance. The woman staring back looked patient. Polished. Impeccably intact. The bitterness she felt beneath the surface didn't show—she wouldn't let it. Bitterness was a luxury she only indulged in private, like an expensive liquor poured into a cut-crystal glass and savored slowly. It was a private pleasure, a righteous indulgence she didn't have to explain or excuse.

Her ex-husband had cheated on her—not once, but many times. The betrayal hadn't come with shouting or tears. It came like a bruise she didn't notice until she pressed on it—subtle, spreading, irreversible. She had believed he loved her and only wanted her. She trusted him, and she poured all of herself into that marriage. She'd made the home beautiful, the dinners exquisite, the sex fulfilling. She knew that no other woman could ever match her impeccable taste in everything from music to literature to food and wine and art. She was beautiful, talented, cultured, intelligent, and devastatingly elegant.

Their sex life had been abundant, intense, alive. Her appetite for intimacy had matched his—or so she thought. Her husband should not have wanted anything more than her, nor anything less.

When she ended her marriage, instead of feeling loss, she felt exhilarated. A rush of clarity. As though the shackles had fallen from her ankles and she could finally walk without dragging dead weight. It wasn't grief she felt—it was awakening. A flame rekindled after years of cold.

Even so, her anger and bitterness never waned. She carried them through her life like a souvenir. A warning. A charm. A scar that glimmered under her silk blouse, visible only to those who knew where to look. To remind her that no matter how much she gives, it will only ever be taken. And she wanted to keep that knowledge for herself. Let it be her edge. Her armor. Her blade.

Mark. Meredith had always thought Mark was one of the good ones too. Not only was he good-looking, but he was somewhat successful, and from what she could tell—at least from outward appearances—he portrayed a good father, a good husband. The kind of man women pointed to at dinner parties and said, "Now that's a catch." But now? Now, she wasn't surprised to learn he was just another narcissist who wanted to take whatever he could.

Claire broke herself to keep everything perfect. Bent over backwards. Lost herself in the act of trying to please a man who would never be satisfied.

And for what?

Men like him were a virus—dull, entitled, rewarded anyway. And women, good women, bled themselves dry trying to stay small enough to be loved by them. They folded themselves into paper dolls, hoping to be held instead of torn.

It was a game Meredith had watched her entire life, and she was done pretending not to see the rules. Let Claire keep chasing scraps of affection if she wanted. Let her stay curled in the corner of a crumbling marriage, hoping to be noticed.

Meredith had long since stopped mistaking survival for devotion.

She had no interest in being admired for her patience. She wanted to be envied for her power.

She walked into her study, the quietest room in the house, and curled up on the large burgundy velvet loveseat with her fresh glass of wine. The fabric sighed beneath her as she sank into it, one leg folded beneath the other, fingers curling around the stem of the glass. The air here smelled faintly of cedar and old pages—a scent she had grown to associate with solace, with command. This was her sanctuary, the place where she let the mask slip—only slightly, only when no one was watching.

Her gaze drifted toward the photo on the walnut bookshelf. It was a picture of herself with her husband. They were on vacation in the South of France, smiling against a backdrop of pale sky and wine-dark sea. Her skin was golden, her hair kissed by salt and wind. Her eyes sparkled with an ease she hadn't felt in years. She would never have guessed that just a few days before that photo had been taken, he'd been with someone else. Someone younger. Someone less.

She breathed in deep through her nose and exhaled slowly. Then, without hurry, she wiped a single tear from her cheek with the back of her hand, not out of grief, but something closer to contempt. It wasn't sadness that made her cry. It was memory. Memory with sharp edges.

Women—especially women who were accomplished, beautiful, and smart—were chronically unappreciated. They were adored until they became inconvenient. Worshipped until they asked for more. Replaced without hesitation. It was the oldest story in the book, dressed up in modern clothes. Meredith had lived it. Watched her mother live it. Seen it stitched into the quiet wounds of every woman she admired.

She had been a good wife. Not just good—exceptional. Loyal without becoming dull. Elegant without arrogance. Sensual without compromise. And still, he had wanted something else. Or maybe not even something—just newness. Novelty. The sick addiction to possibility.

Her glass tipped slightly, wine swirling red as blood. She stared at it a long time. And then, with the faintest curl of her mouth—an expression too subtle to be called a smile, too precise to be called a smirk—she whispered to herself, almost like a lullaby, each syllable deliberate:

"A good wife deserves better."

Then she leaned back, let her head rest against the cushion, and stared at the ceiling as if waiting for the stars to answer.

Chapter Eleven

The Trap

The plan had to be precise, every detail executed with the cold calculation of a surgeon's blade—controlled, undetectable, and final, like venom slipped seamlessly into a delicate cup of tea, sweet enough to disguise its intent but fatal just the same. It wasn't just strategy—it was survival, wrapped in silk and carried in silence. This wasn't about fear anymore. It wasn't about evasion or endurance or even redemption. It was about bait. About flipping the narrative. About luring the thing that hunted her out of the shadows and into the open.

It felt almost like planning a heist—deliberate, methodical, tinged with the same electric charge of risk that once used to flutter in her chest when she walked into unfamiliar hotel rooms under a name that wasn't hers. But this wasn't theft, and it certainly wasn't surrender. It was something else entirely. Something colder. This was an invitation. A signal flare. If whoever was behind the warnings wanted her attention, they would have it—on her terms, in her arena, with her watching every move.

She moved through the house with quiet purpose, a kind of sterile grace, her bare feet soundless against the hardwood as she crossed into the kitchen. She retrieved the burner phone from the drawer where it had been sleeping like a loaded weapon and opened the most recent thread, her thumb hovering briefly before she began to type. Each word felt like a needle threading its way into skin—measured, final, sharp.

"Let's meet. Same hotel. Room 620. 1 p.m. Today. No games."

She read it twice before pressing send, and even then, her breath caught high in her chest, as though the air had thickened around her. She didn't allow herself to linger on the screen. Instead, she powered the phone down, removed the SIM card, and walked briskly to the garage.

On the workbench, beside a tangle of forgotten holiday lights and a rusted wrench, she placed the burner phone on an old dish towel and brought the hammer down hard. Once. Twice. Three times. The screen spidered instantly, plastic cracking like brittle bone. She didn't flinch. She dropped the fractured pieces into a ziplock bag, sealed it, then slipped that inside another, wrapping it tight as though containing a contagion.

Back in the kitchen, she buried the bag deep in the trash beneath wet coffee grounds, wilted lettuce, and half a cracked eggshell. The garbage bag was already heavy, but she lifted it in one motion, tied it with two tight knots, and carried it outside, where she dropped it into the black bin at the end of the driveway with a satisfying thud. When she shut the lid, her hands were shaking. Her breath hadn't returned to normal. It felt like she was already running.

The house was still and silent when she stepped back inside, but Claire didn't let herself pause. She moved with the precision of someone enacting a plan rehearsed only in the dark corners of her mind. There could be no missteps. No hesitation.

Upstairs, she opened her closet, selecting clothes with clinical detachment. She chose pieces that were deliberately unremarkable: baggy jeans that sagged slightly at the knees, an oatmeal-colored sweater whose stretched collar and pilled sleeves made her look smaller, muted. Invisible. Her hair she scraped back into a low, blunt ponytail, secured with a dull clip. A quick swipe of tinted moisturizer, the faintest brush of mascara. No earrings. No lipstick. No rings. She studied her reflection with a kind of cold detachment. Today, she would not be Claire Holloway. Today, she would be no one.

She left her phone on the kitchen counter, face-down, as though it too needed to be silenced. She got into the Subaru—the spare car that smelled faintly of campfire and old Cheerios, she hadn't used it in months. She drove three blocks from the hotel and parked it on a side street beneath a swaying oak. Her boots made no sound as she crossed the cracked pavement, then the sidewalk, head bowed slightly, pace deliberate but unhurried. She tied her shoe once. Crossed the street again. Checked every reflection in passing windows. If someone was watching, they would see only a tired woman with a long day ahead. They would see someone forgettable. Someone unimportant. That was the idea.

She slipped into the Mason Hill Suites through the same side entrance as before, the one near the rarely used conference rooms that always smelled faintly of mothballs and resignation. The carpet hadn't changed—still that lurid plum hue that managed to feel both garish and weary, like it had absorbed decades of bad decisions. The lemon-scented disinfectant hung heavy in the air, masking something older, something darker—a musty undertone of mildew and memory that clung to the back of her throat. Claire moved quickly but without drawing attention, her gaze steady, her pulse thudding in her ears like a metronome set just a notch too fast.

The elevator yawned open as if expecting her, and she stepped inside, pressing the button for the sixth floor with the flat of her knuckle. She did not glance at her reflection in the mirrored walls. She didn't need to. She already knew what she looked like: a shadow of herself, stripped down to the outline of a woman too careful to leave a trace.

The doors closed with a soft hiss, and the numbers blinked upward in silence—three, four, five—each floor a held breath. She counted the seconds automatically, the same way she had a year ago: fourteen from lobby to six. Some strange comfort in the consistency, in the illusion that time hadn't warped everything. When the elevator dinged, she stepped out into the hallway with the posture of someone with a destination, even though she had none.

Room 620 was ahead on the left, three doors from the elevator bank. She passed it without pausing, her pace deliberate but measured, and slipped into the recessed alcove near the vending machines and ice bucket station. It smelled of artificial cherry and stale air. She leaned casually against the wall, pretending to scroll through her nonexistent phone, eyes fixed just enough on the patterned carpet to avoid suspicion, ears attuned to the slightest sound—footsteps, voices, the mechanical clunk of a door latch turning.

Nothing came at first—no footsteps, no sounds beyond the faraway hum of a vacuum on another floor and the metallic rattle of the ice machine cycling. Claire kept her posture loose, but her mind was tightly wound, every nerve strained like piano wire. The silence stretched, taut and unforgiving, broken only by the occasional ping of the elevator or the rustle of housekeeping carts. Twenty-two minutes passed, each one a slow drip of adrenaline, until the stillness began to feel staged. Manufactured. She began to wonder if it had all been for nothing—if she'd fallen into some paranoid loop, chasing ghosts conjured by exhaustion and fear. Her muscles began to ache from holding still. Doubt crept in like a draft under the door. Maybe she'd imagined everything. Maybe the texts were long deleted for a reason. Maybe no one was coming.

Then came the elevator ding.

A soft chime, no louder than a throat cleared in a chapel, but it might as well have been a gunshot. Claire's spine straightened instinctively, her breath locking in her chest. She didn't move. Didn't breathe. Waited. She strained her

155

ears for movement, her heart pulsing in her throat. For several seconds, there was nothing. No footsteps. No voices. Just the whir of the elevator doors sliding closed again—and then, at last, the echo of steps. Deliberate. Heavy. Slow enough to register, quick enough to cover ground. Claire shifted her weight infinitesimally to the left, just enough to catch a sliver of movement through the narrow seam between the alcove wall and the vending machine. A figure came into view. Tall. Broad. A gray coat hung past the waist. A baseball cap, brim pulled low. His hands stayed in his pockets. He didn't pause outside Room 620. Didn't glance at it. Instead, he approached the fire escape map mounted on the far wall—studied it, as if lost. Then, without urgency, he turned.

And looked straight at her.

Claire didn't move. Didn't blink. Her back pressed flatter against the cold wall, her fingers curled into fists so tight her nails bit crescents into her palms.

She couldn't see him fully—just a partial profile obscured by the cap's shadow, the briefest flick of his eyes. But she knew. Not from the shape of his face, which remained hidden, or the color of his coat, which was unremarkable, but from the way he looked at her with knowledge. Recognition. Calculation. The same look he'd given her in the produce aisle, barely perceptible and yet unforgettable.

That impossible weight of being seen, really seen, by someone you didn't even know you knew. He was holding something that looked like a weapon, she was sure. And he was planning on using it.

He didn't say a word. He turned and walked briskly down the hallway towards her like he had every right to be there. Like he had every right to her.

She froze for a few seconds, each one stretching out like a blade held against her skin—before her body remembered how to move. He was getting closer. She sprang from the alcove without looking back, her flats barely touching the carpet as she sprinted past the closed doors, breath caught somewhere between her chest and throat. She hit the stairwell door so hard it banged against the wall, echoing down the concrete shaft like a gunshot. The elevator was a trap now. Too slow. Too exposed. She took the stairs two at a time, her legs trembling under the force of her descent, one hand skimming the rail for balance, the other clenched around nothing at all. She didn't stop, didn't stumble, not until she reached the lobby level, her lungs heaving, her vision swimming with panic.

She didn't exit through the main lobby. She couldn't. Her instincts screamed against it, warning her that if she stepped into the light now—through those polished brass doors and beneath the artificial smile of the awning—she'd be seen, maybe followed, maybe caught. Instead, she veered left, into the conference wing, ducking through the dim corridor lined with beige doors and generic art. Her footsteps echoed unevenly against the tile, faster now, erratic. At the end of the hallway, she found the side door to the parking garage and shoved through it, spilling into the low-ceilinged concrete gloom. The air smelled of gasoline, damp stone, and exhaust. Claire stumbled on a slick patch of oil, her knee slamming into the ground hard enough to jolt her spine. She hissed, staggered to her feet, and kept moving.

Her breaths came in short, ragged bursts now, each one sharp enough to sting her throat as she raced toward the car. Her footsteps slapped the concrete, echoing in staccato bursts as she wove between parked cars, ducking behind a dusty sedan to scan her surroundings. No footsteps behind her. No voices. No shadow moving in the dim fluorescents. But that didn't mean she was alone. Her hand trembled as she reached for her keys, fumbling with the fob before the familiar chirp of the old Subaru echoed back at her. She yanked the door open, threw herself inside, and locked the doors with a shaky jab of her thumb. Only then, sealed inside the cabin, did her body finally respond to the terror she'd kept caged inside: a scream tore its way from her chest, hoarse and guttural and entirely involuntary.

She gripped the steering wheel with both hands, her fingers stiff and white as bone, the vinyl slick beneath her damp palms. For a moment she couldn't move. Couldn't think. The garage lights hummed overhead, flickering slightly. She stared straight ahead, chest heaving, her pulse throbbing in her ears like the bass line of some slow, inevitable song.

Claire pulled into the driveway just as the last of the daylight collapsed behind the trees, the sky bruised purple and gold. Her hands were still trembling on the steering wheel, the outline of that hotel hallway burned into her vision. She sat in the car for a full minute before moving, her breath fogging faintly against the windshield. Everything inside her wanted to race inside, bolt the doors, double-check the windows— but something else, something quieter and more deliberate, made her pause.

The mailbox stood like a sentinel at the end of the path, matte black and undisturbed. But as Claire stepped out, gravel crunching beneath her shoes, she noticed the slot wasn't fully closed. Her heart stuttered. She forced herself forward, one step at a time, a warning bell screaming behind her ribs.

She opened the lid.

Inside was a single envelope—cream-colored, thick, her name handwritten across the front in ink that bled slightly into the paper as if written in haste. There was no stamp. No return address.

Just her.

Claire's fingers hovered for a moment before she reached in and took it. The weight of the envelope sent a cold shiver up her arm. She turned toward the house, walking faster now, urgency mounting with every step.

Inside, she locked the door with trembling hands and tore the envelope open in the foyer, ignoring her coat, her bag, everything else. A single photo slid out. It wasn't glossy—more like a print from a low-grade surveillance camera—but the image was clear enough.

Her.

From behind.

Running.

Down the hallway of the Mason Hill Suites.

She recognized the sweater instantly, the slouch of her shoulders, the panic in her stride. It was from that afternoon. The moment she thought she'd escaped.

She flipped it over.

On the back, in the same ink, was a single word:

TRAPPED.

Claire staggered back, the envelope fluttering to the floor like a dead leaf. Her pulse thundered in her ears. He had been behind her. He had been close enough to capture her. Close enough to choose not to touch her. Not yet.

Because this wasn't about hurting her.

It was about control.

And he had it.

The photo. The hallway. That single word—TRAPPED. Her thoughts spun wildly, latching onto fragments, desperate for logic where there was none. He had been behind her. He had followed her. He had taken her picture. And then he delivered it to her mail before she could even get home. Which meant—he had never stopped watching.

The realization settled over her like a second skin—tight, suffocating, inescapable. Every step she had taken that day, every calculated choice, every careful disguise—it had all been observed, anticipated, undone before she even knew she was being hunted. She had thought she was the one laying the trap, pulling the strings, reclaiming power on her terms. But now, with that single image in her trembling hands, it was clear: she hadn't been the hunter. She had been the bait. And the game had already begun without her consent.

She stood in the entryway, motionless, the photo still in her hand, the edges crumpling beneath her tightening grip. The light overhead flickered once, then steadied. Every sound in the house was suddenly too loud—the hum of the refrigerator, the slow tick of the wall clock, the faint creak of old wood settling beneath its own weight. She turned in a slow circle, eyes scanning corners she knew were empty, but still didn't trust.

Her heartbeat throbbed in her throat, an arrhythmic drum she couldn't silence.

She should call someone. Meredith, maybe. But the moment she thought of picking up the phone, her stomach turned.

There was no one to call. No one she trusted enough. No one who wouldn't ask questions she wasn't ready to answer.

She crossed the room, set the photo facedown on the kitchen counter, and reached for the light switch. She flicked it off, then on again. Just to feel the power respond. Just to remind herself that she still had some measure of control in this house, even if it was just the lights.

But the truth pressed in from every wall: she wasn't setting the trap anymore.

She was the one caught inside it.

Chapter Twelve

The Handler

He had always loved the moment just before the scream—the breathless instant when a woman's instincts kicked in and her spine stiffened, when the tilt of her head or the narrowing of her eyes betrayed the flicker of fear before it could become sound. That sliver of silence was delicious, sharpened by the knowledge that she didn't yet know what was coming, only that something was wrong. Fear, when you learned how to listen for it, could be its own kind of music. And Jeff had become a virtuoso.

He sat parked across the street from Oakridge Elementary in an unmarked charcoal sedan, its engine purring with a low, velvety hum like an animal crouched in tall grass. One hand rested idly on the steering wheel, the other curled loosely in his lap, fingers twitching with anticipation. He wasn't here for the girls. Watching them—Emma and Sadie, all wide eyes and bubble jackets—was a formality, a flex of control, a reminder. The truth was simpler and crueler: he wanted Claire to know that he *could* be here for them. That the boundary between her life and his wasn't a wall, but a thread—and it was already fraying.

She had always been too composed for his liking, too poised, too proud of her reinvention. Claire Holloway. The picturesque suburban wife with a neat little life and a designer bag. But that's not who she really was. He knew better. She had been Delia once. And no matter how many casseroles she made or volunteer forms she signed, Delia still lived under her skin like rot beneath polished wood.

She thought she'd escaped. Thought she'd been clever. She thought her secrets had been buried under fresh paint and seasonal wreaths and chamomile tea. But she had forgotten one important thing: Jeff was the one who had built Delia. He'd shaped her from nothing. Given her purpose, connections, power. He had made her—and he still owned her.

From behind the smudged windshield, Jeff watched as teachers ushered clusters of children out to waiting minivans. Mothers in leggings clutched backpacks to their chests like makeshift shields, scanning the crowd for their own. No one gave him a second glance. They never did. A clean-shaven man in a department-issued windbreaker, badge clipped to his belt, the weary air of someone overworked and underpaid. Harmless. Official. Invisible.

He was not, strictly speaking, a real detective. He had the credentials—just enough to flash when necessary—and he knew the scripts. He'd taken the classes, earned the certificates, worn the uniform once or twice when it suited him. But it wasn't justice he loved. It wasn't order. It was the power people gave so easily to anyone who pretended to protect them. A badge opened doors. It sealed lips. It turned suspicion into compliance with a single flick of laminated plastic. He didn't need a weapon when the world gave him permission with a smile.

The burner buzzed against his thigh—just once. No message. No call. A phantom tremor, like a nerve twitch or a warning bell. It meant she was spiraling now. He had gotten inside. The panic had begun.

Claire Holloway was unraveling.

And it was exquisite.

She didn't yet know how far he had reached into her world—how precisely, how patiently. Each breadcrumb he had left behind was placed with deliberate care. The lipstick stained teacup on the kitchen counter. The hotel key card slipped under her door. The anonymous matchbook with a message scrawled in that unmistakable ink. The photo tucked into her mailbox. The radio static whispering her old name. Every item was surgical in its effect. Too specific to be random. Too intimate to ignore.

He hadn't rushed a single step. Claire wasn't the kind of woman you could break with blunt force. She required nuance. Subtlety. A long, cold campaign of psychological erosion. She had to feel the tremor in her gut before the quake. She had to be the one to tear her own life apart, piece by careful piece. He didn't need to touch her to destroy her.

He only needed to make her doubt everything—her safety, her memories, her marriage, even herself.

Hotel surveillance meant nothing to him. He'd spent years studying vulnerabilities in camera loops, access logs, Wi-Fi drops. Room 604 never caught his face because he'd spliced the hallway feed. Hotel systems were children's toys—

plastic and fragile. He knew where the wires crossed, which ports failed, when to hold still and when to strike. Radio signals, too, bent for him. That whisper she heard through the kitchen speaker—"Delia…"—that hadn't been a ghost. That had been Jeff. Frequency manipulation and a modified transmitter slipped behind a pantry outlet. A parlor trick to anyone who understood waveform latency. But to her, it was terror incarnate.

The cameras he'd planted inside her home had been even easier. Less than forty minutes while she was out—he timed it to coincide with the girls' swim practice and Mark's standing Tuesday meeting. He let himself in through the side utility panel, bypassing the security system with a universal keypad decrypter and a steady hand. One camera nestled discreetly in the upstairs smoke detector. Another behind the vent grille in the master bedroom. A third disguised as the binding of a book in the study, tucked between "Wuthering Heights" and "Braving the Wilderness." She'd never notice. Most people didn't read what they displayed.

Now, he could see everything. Her pacing in the hallway at 2 a.m., the way she stood frozen in front of the door before checking the locks one more time. The trembling fingers she pressed to her lips when she thought no one was watching.

He catalogued her movements the way an artist studies brushstrokes—every flicker of doubt, every instinctual twitch. And when she was calm for too long, he'd stir the water. Switch the girls' show to something dark. Leave the front door open just enough to make her wonder. Haunt her with questions that had no answers.

It wasn't about hurting her. Not directly.

It was about making her feel hunted.

Making her question reality.

Making her remember who was in control.

Claire's punishment, in Jeff's mind, had been decided long ago—etched into the wallpaper of Room 604 like a curse. That afternoon should have ended her story. That hotel room wasn't merely a scene; it had been a crucible. She was meant to vanish afterward. Delia gone. Claire dissolved. Nothing left behind but a mystery and a memory. She was supposed to understand the message: when you walked away from the deal, you didn't get to walk away clean.

He remembered the way she'd said it over the burner phone, voice perfectly measured: "I'm done." She had said she was ready to bury Delia for good, to retire the name like a costume she'd grown out of. He'd let her say the words. Let her believe she had power. That's what he did. He listened. He made them feel heard. And then he rewrote the ending.

By the time he arrived at Room 604, he already knew everything he needed to. David Holbrook hadn't been some innocent banker with a secret. He'd used a fake last name—booked with cash, kept his profile sanitized—but Jeff had unraveled it within a day. Not for professional reasons. For personal ones. Because Delia had raised concerns. "This one's different," she'd said. "Something's off." And Jeff, for the first time in a long while, had looked beyond the transaction.

167

What he discovered was worse than he expected.

David Holbrook was his brother-in-law.

Jeff's sister had married him eight years prior. A high society wedding in Savannah, silver invitations, five-piece quartet, the works. Jeff had hated him from the beginning. Holbrook had the kind of smile that looked practiced in the mirror. Too clean, too cold. And when Jeff told his sister— quietly, carefully, that David was seeing escorts—she didn't ask how he knew. She just looked at him, flat and dry-eyed, and said, "Take care of it. Both of them. Him and the whore." He hadn't hesitated.

Room 604 had always been a setup—carefully, cruelly designed. Claire thought she was there for closure, for a final job, but she had unknowingly walked into someone else's revenge. Jeff arrived minutes after she stepped out. He passed her in the hallway, her face turned away, her steps hurried. He could've reached out, touched her wrist, stopped her. But he didn't. There was no need to rush what was already in motion.

David was alone inside, drunk, sitting in the bed clothed from the waist down and drinking scotch. He looked up when Jeff entered—no alarm, no confusion, just that bored arrogance that made Jeff's blood simmer. "Finally," David muttered, thinking it was Delia returning. He didn't even bother checking.

Jeff didn't answer. Didn't say a word. He scanned the room once, calmly, methodically. The tie discarded on the dresser. The envelope of money next to it. The glass, half-full again.

Then he moved—silent, fluid—as though the whole thing were choreography. The crystal vase stood on the sideboard, weighty and decorative. Useless, except for this one moment. When he brought it down, it made a sound that felt like finality—a wet crack followed by a silence that bloomed like smoke. He brought it down twice more.

David hit the floor without ceremony. No scream. No warning. Just the sudden, brutal end of breath.

Jeff watched him twitch for a moment, the blood already darkening the cheap carpet beneath his temple. He felt no satisfaction. Just completion. A task resolved.

And then the door opened.

Delia—Claire—stood there, one foot still in the hallway, her face unreadable. She didn't scream. She didn't run. She looked at the body. Then at the envelope.

And she took it.

Her fingers moved with elegance, not greed. She picked up the cash and slipped it into her bag like she was collecting dry cleaning. He thought maybe she would say something, but she didn't. She just turned and walked out, never looking back.

He had let her go.

And he didn't know why.

He told himself it was because she hadn't flinched. Because there had been something in her eyes—an understanding, maybe, or something worse. Something that mirrored him. Not fear. Not horror. Recognition. For a while, that had earned her his silence.

But silence had a shelf life.

And now, watching her pretend to be someone else—baking muffins, sweeping porches, folding school newsletters like they were sacred—was becoming intolerable. She had taken the life he was supposed to take from her and made it look like redemption. She was a wife, a mother, a woman the world trusted, when in his mind, she was still a weapon. A well-dressed illusion. She didn't get to disappear into perfection. Not without his permission.

Jeff parked two blocks down and waited. He knew she was home. He knew the girls were out.

He rolled down the window, let the summer air drift in. It carried hints of fresh-cut grass, charcoal smoke, and something sour beneath it. Rot, maybe. Or guilt. He closed his eyes and listened—to the dogs barking down the street, the metallic click of someone's gate latching, the gentle whir of a lawn sprinkler hitting pavement.

Every sound had meaning if you paid close enough attention.

From the glovebox, he retrieved another envelope. This one thicker than the last, padded with images. Claire in her kitchen. Claire standing at the sink. Claire through the second-story window, head bowed in what looked like prayer.

She didn't know yet what he'd taken from her.

She didn't know how thoroughly she'd already been broken open.

He turned the key in the ignition with a movement so casual it belied the meticulous violence of his thoughts, the steady hum of the engine masking the darker rhythm inside him.

He drove slowly, deliberately, down the street, the car coasting like a predator mid-stalk.

Two blocks from Claire's house, he parked and cut the engine, letting the silence settle around him like fog. He didn't move right away. Just sat there, eyes fixed on the outline of her house in the distance, windows glowing faintly in the soft bleed of early evening. The neighborhood was quiet, picturesque—yards trimmed, porches swept, the illusion of peace wrapped tightly around every fence post. But he knew better. He knew what lay beneath perfection. Rot. Guilt. Secrets desperate to stay buried.

She was already inside, locking doors with trembling fingers, checking windows twice, unaware that nothing she could bolt would matter. Fear had its own keys. It knew every way in. And she was already dreaming in static—he could see it. The way she moved in stilted rhythms now, glancing behind her more often, second-guessing every sound. She wasn't breaking yet, but she was cracking. Slowly. Deliciously. He had her right where he wanted her.

171

Jeff didn't believe in chaos. Chaos was for amateurs—messy, loud, too easily traced. What he believed in was orchestration. A symphony of unease, every note intentional. In the basement of his home—a modest, unremarkable rental no one would ever suspect—he kept boxes. Not clutter. Not memorabilia. Records. Evidence. Artifacts. He had printed emails, encrypted flash drives, transcribed conversations. He had maps marked with dates and times, receipts, surveillance logs. Claire's schedule. Her daughters' names.

The old hotels she'd once frequented under different aliases. He even had a sample of her handwriting, the way she curled her L's when signing for room service.

He knew the pace of her footsteps when she was anxious. He knew the scent of her shampoo, the way her breathing changed when she lied. His collection was not obsession. It was ownership. And Claire, no matter what name she used, still belonged to him.

He had loved managing those women—not because he desired them, not in the crude, predictable way people might assume, but because of the control it afforded him. The duality of power and permission.

They feared him and trusted him in the same breath, a perfect contradiction he had cultivated with care. Claire had been the most fascinating. The most contained. The one who always followed the rules but never once made herself vulnerable. She was a ghost in designer heels, gliding between transactions like a wisp of smoke. But even smoke could leave behind a scent. And now, watching her from his car as she moved through her kitchen—chopping vegetables, folding napkins, adjusting her daughters' backpacks—he could see it: the tremor just beneath her surface. She was unraveling. Slowly. Elegantly. Just the way he liked it.

She moved like she was still trying to hold the illusion together—precise in her gestures, controlled in her expressions—but he knew better. He could see it in the way her hand hovered a beat too long over the faucet handle, how her shoulders stiffened when she passed the hallway mirror, how she paused at the base of the stairs, listening.

Claire wasn't just scared—she was changing. Fear had begun to calcify into something sharper. But it was too late. She was already playing his game. Already walking his labyrinth. He didn't need to touch her to break her; he just had to watch. And wait. And remind her, over and over again, that she was never out of reach.

Every move she made now bore the mark of someone being watched—measured, rehearsed, slightly too careful. He could almost hear her thoughts, ticking like a metronome: Check the locks. Close the blinds. Count the steps from the window to the stairs. She was living like prey, and he had no intention of letting her forget it. Control was never about force—it was about presence. About threading himself into her daily rituals so seamlessly that even her coffee tasted like caution.

He didn't bother entering her house again that night. He didn't need to. The fear was already thick in her bloodstream, already beginning to distort her sleep, her instincts, her ability to think clearly. And that was the goal.

Not chaos, not blood. Only erosion—slow, deliberate erosion. He would take from her what she cherished most: control.

Back in his apartment—clean, featureless, the kind of place that left no impression—Jeff settled into the leather chair by the window. He lit a cigarette and opened his laptop. The monitors blinked awake. One camera showed Claire in the hallway, another captured her in the kitchen, a third held her motionless in the living room, curled beneath a gray blanket, holding her knees. She was still wearing the oatmeal sweater.

He smirked.

He watched her check the locks again. Watched her mouth something—maybe a prayer, maybe a curse. Watched her pause at the window and press her hand against the glass like she was trying to sense something on the other side. She was exhausted. She was furious. She was exquisite.

He leaned back in the chair, exhaled a slow stream of smoke, and smiled—not because he'd won, but because she hadn't realized yet that she was never going to.

This was his masterpiece.

And she, whether she liked it or not, was his canvas.

Chapter Thirteen

The Undoing

There was a pause after breakfast—an almost imperceptible hesitation as Mark rinsed his plate, set it in the dishwasher, and closed the door too gently.

That softness, the false quiet in his movement, told Claire everything. It wasn't calm. It was calculation. It was the practiced choreography of a man hiding something.

The sound of the dishwasher latch locking into place was too quiet to echo, but it landed in her ears with surgical precision, crisp and final. A deliberate silence fell across the kitchen, the kind that drew sharp edges around every detail—the low hum of the refrigerator, the faint tick of the wall clock, the lazy drip of water from the edge of the faucet that hadn't been shut all the way. Morning light slanted through the wide windows above the sink, making the granite countertops gleam unnaturally clean. The air itself felt weighted, suspended between what had just passed and what hadn't yet been said.

She stood on the other side of the kitchen island, fingers curled around a coffee mug gone cold long ago.

The ceramic had long since lost its warmth, but her grip remained tight, as though the act of holding it rooted her to the moment. She focused on the chipped edge near the rim, her eyes tracing the faint web of a crack beneath the glaze, unable to lift her gaze to the man moving too quietly in front of her. Mark's back remained rigid, his shoulders squared with a tension she had come to recognize as effortful restraint. He didn't look at her. Not once.

"Is there something wrong?" she asked.

Her voice was quiet, measured—held between the lines of curiosity and accusation—but it still felt loud in the sterile space between them.

He dried his hands too slowly. The hand towel dragged across his palms in methodical passes, as if he were buying time. "No."

The lie lingered.

"You've barely spoken to me in three days."

Her words didn't rise in pitch. They came out flat, almost clinical, which only made them more severe. She had rehearsed the line in her mind too many times to infuse it with anything like surprise. Her breath shortened. She held it and then released it too quickly, the air escaping in a way that made her feel exposed.

He finally turned, leaning one hip against the counter, arms folded. The way he looked at her then—detached, unreadable, like she was a stranger who'd asked too intimate a question—made her chest tighten.

There was no trace of warmth in his face. No recognition. Just the indifferent mask of a man who had already walked too far away.

"I'm tired," he said. "And I don't feel like having this conversation."

His tone was clipped but not cruel, deliberately neutral, which somehow cut deeper. He wasn't reacting in anger. He was simply disengaging.

"This conversation?" Her voice was shaking now. "You mean the one where I ask what's happening to us and you shut it down like I'm imagining things?"

The quiver caught her by surprise. Her body betrayed her, betraying the effort she had put into holding everything in check. It cracked at the edge of her words. She fought the heat building at the base of her neck.

Mark rolled his eyes. "Here we go."

The sound of her mug hitting the counter was sharp and final. Claire set it down harder than she meant to.

The sound made him glance down briefly, but he said nothing.

"No, say it. Go ahead. Roll your eyes. Treat me like I'm crazy. But you haven't touched me in weeks. You're either gone or silent or looking through me like I'm nothing."

The air seemed to ripple slightly around her, like the temperature had changed even though nothing had shifted. Her stomach tensed. Her nails dug into the side of the island.

He laughed—quiet, joyless. "Maybe I'm just tired of pretending."

The words hit her like open palm to cheek.

There was no rise in his voice, no gesture. He simply let

the words drop between them and fall where they may.

She took a step back. "Pretending what?" Mark stared at her.

Said nothing.

Seconds passed.

"Mark," she whispered. "What are you pretending?"

Her throat constricted. She tasted salt already, though no tears had fallen yet. The walls of the kitchen closed in an inch.

He hesitated just long enough to twist the knife. "That we're fine. That any of this is normal."

Claire's head tilted slightly, as if trying to balance the weight of his words in her mind. She swallowed hard, but the lump in her throat remained.

She felt the tears rise before she could stop them. "Then why stay? If I make you so miserable—why not just leave?"

His jaw tightened. The skin around his mouth drew in, his lips pressed into a thin, exhausted line.

"Because I have daughters. Because I've built a life I'm not ready to burn down. Because maybe I was hoping you'd stop acting so fucking suspicious all the time."

Her mouth parted. She blinked. The breath she'd pulled in caught halfway.

"Suspicious?"

The word emerged with a different kind of tone now— sharper, bewildered. Her pulse pounded against the hollow of her throat.

"You don't think I notice?" He stepped forward now, his voice low and sharp. "You disappearing during the day. That night you went to the hotel and lied about it. The way you flinch when I walk into a room, like I'm the threat. You've been different, Claire. You've been... hiding."

His eyes didn't shift. They bore into her with a coldness she hadn't seen before. It was unnerving. Not loud. Not overtly threatening. Just… immovable.

She opened her mouth, then closed it again. Her lips parted, but the words caught and tangled, refusing to surface.

He leaned closer. "Are you seeing someone?"

"What?"

"Is that what this is?" His tone was laced with something sour. "All this paranoia, the crying, the mood swings. Are you fucking someone else?"

The slap she imagined didn't happen. But it flashed behind her eyes—fast, bright.

Her voice trembled under the weight of everything she couldn't say. "No," she said. "I'm not."

"Then tell me why you were at the Mason Hill Suites." Her

legs went weak.

She felt her knees subtly buckle beneath her, the room tilting just enough to require the steadying grip of her hand on the marble countertop. The name of the hotel had fallen from his mouth like a challenge. Her heart thundered. Her vision blurred for a moment at the edges.

"I saw the parking charge on the card," he said, folding his arms again. "You didn't mention it. You didn't say a word." She struggled to breathe evenly. The oxygen she pulled into her lungs felt sharp, metallic. "I wasn't—God, Mark. I wasn't meeting anyone."

"Then what were you doing there?"

She reached for the nearest lie. "I was sitting in the parking lot. I needed a minute to myself. I was overwhelmed and I didn't want the girls to see me fall apart."

The silence that followed was not acceptance. It was evaluation.

He narrowed his eyes.

"I haven't been well," she added quickly. "I'm tired. I'm sad. I don't sleep anymore. And I've been trying to pretend like everything's okay for your sake. For theirs."

Mark watched her a long moment, expression unreadable.

He blinked once, slow and deliberate. "You think I believe that?"

"I don't care if you do," she whispered. "It's the truth." She turned away then, because if she kept looking at him, she would start screaming or sobbing or both. She walked upstairs. Shut the bedroom door behind her. Locked it.

And cried into a towel so the girls wouldn't hear.

The fights came in waves.

Some started with a word. Others with a silence. He accused her of keeping secrets. She accused him of withholding love. Neither said what they really meant.

It didn't begin as a storm, but as tremors—subtle shifts in mood that rippled beneath the surface of their daily routine.

The kind of unease that filled a room before a glass ever shattered. One morning, Mark asked why the girls' permission slips hadn't been signed. Claire's voice cracked when she answered. That evening, he sighed when she reminded him about the PTA meeting, and she took the sigh as an indictment. They moved around each other with brittle choreography, the air between them thick with misinterpretations.

Mark's cruelty was quiet, but it cut.

He didn't yell. He didn't raise a hand. He made observations. Just soft enough to sound reasonable. Just sharp enough to draw blood. He'd glance at her empty coffee mug and say, "Did you eat anything today?" His tone feigned concern, but she heard the undercurrent—*you're falling apart.* When she forgot to pack Emma's lunch, he held the brown paper bag up between two fingers and asked, "Is something going on with you?" in front of the girls.

When Sadie's ballet shoes were still in the backseat on recital night, he sighed audibly and said he'd "take care of it," like she was the child.

He called it concern. But she could see the judgment in every glance.

He'd come home later and later, the sound of the garage door grinding open at the edge of bedtime, long after dinner had

been cleared and the dishwasher run. His excuses were flimsy—late meetings, traffic, a colleague's emergency—but she stopped asking. He didn't bother with details. He didn't need to. The gap between them was widening too fast to fill with anything like conversation.

His absences grew longer. His texts shorter. Sometimes she'd catch him staring into his phone with a strange look on his face—not anger, not distraction—just distance. Like his mind lived somewhere else now, and she was no longer even a blip on the map.

He left rooms when she entered them. He stayed seated when she walked by. He shut doors that used to stay open.

Once, she stood outside their bedroom and listened to him brushing his teeth behind the door he hadn't bothered to leave ajar. A sound so ordinary—bristles against enamel, water running in short bursts—suddenly felt like proof that she'd become unwelcome in her own life.

He was scared.

She saw that now.

He thought she knew something.

And the truth was, she did. Just not what he assumed.

Every time she caught him watching her when he thought she wasn't looking, his expression was too controlled. His movements too slow. There was a calculation in his body language that unsettled her more than anger ever could.

Some nights, she imagined telling him everything. Telling him about the burner phone. The messages. The photograph.

The matchbook. The static voice over the radio. The envelope on the porch. The hotel hallway.

The truth crouched inside her like a coiled animal, restless and heavy. But she couldn't let it out.

Because deep down, she still didn't know if he was part of it.

She lay awake most nights, eyes fixed on the ceiling, listening to him breathe beside her. Wondering if that same breath had been spent on someone else. Wondering if he ever looked at her and still saw the woman he married. Or just a shadow of someone trying too hard to be whole.

The ceiling above their bed was blank and smooth, uncracked and spotless, but night after night she stared at it as though waiting for it to split open and offer her a sign. A word. A way out. When Mark shifted beside her, she stopped breathing. When he spoke her name in the dark, she flinched before answering.

They moved like ghosts. Inhabiting the same rooms. Sleeping in the same bed. Performing the motions of a marriage already gutted of intimacy.

Meredith poured wine and let Claire cry without asking questions.

They were sitting in Meredith's sunroom, the same place Claire had once laughed about dumb Pinterest projects and made plans for a summer trip that now felt like a dream from someone else's life.

The room was still as familiar as ever—soft woven rugs underfoot, oversized linen cushions that retained the gentle impression of where they'd sat last time. The air smelled faintly of lavender and beeswax polish, a scent Meredith always favored. Outside the long bank of windows, a wind stirred the maple trees along the back fence, their rustling branches casting faint, rhythmic shadows that danced across the glass. The overhead fan turned slowly, lazily, keeping the air from going stale. A glass terrarium sat in the corner, half filled with smooth white stones and succulents that always looked slightly thirsty.

Claire sat curled in the same armchair she always chose—second from the right, facing the garden. Her knees were pulled up, bare feet tucked beneath her, the wine glass balanced on her thigh. Her chest still hitched every few breaths, the way it always did after crying. She wiped her eyes with a sleeve, then looked down at her lap, ashamed of how easily she had unraveled.

"He thinks I'm cheating," Claire said.

Her voice was low, nearly inaudible above the whisper of branches against the glass.

Meredith's eyebrows lifted. "Are you?"

The pause that followed wasn't long. But it landed heavily in the space between them.

Claire shot her a look.

Meredith held up one hand in surrender. "Sorry. I just...

Mark is an idiot."

Claire let out a weak laugh. It wasn't humor so much as reflex—an exhausted noise, barely formed.

"He's scared. But he's not saying why."

She took a sip of wine, not tasting it. The rim of the glass left a faint print on her lip, and her fingers trembled slightly where they gripped the stem. She hadn't eaten much that day—maybe nothing. Everything in her body felt both too heavy and too hollow.

"Then he's scared of something he's doing. Not something you are."

Meredith's tone didn't rise. There was no urgency in her voice, just a firm, settled certainty that made Claire's throat tighten.

Claire's throat caught.

The words settled around her shoulders like something warm and unbearable. For a moment, she felt like the child, like the one being protected, the one being reassured. She closed her eyes.

Meredith leaned in. "You've bent yourself backward for that man. You make everything beautiful. You hold everything together. And he doesn't see it. That's not your failure, Claire. That's his."

Claire closed her eyes. "I want to be a good wife. I've tried."

Her voice cracked again, quieter this time, so thin it nearly disappeared into the breeze moving across the windows. "You *are* a good wife," Meredith said firmly. "You just deserve a better husband."

The statement didn't feel like opinion. It felt like verdict.

Claire looked down at her glass, realizing her hands were shaking. She didn't even know why anymore—fear, heartbreak, rage. It all blurred together.

The wine glass wobbled slightly in her grip. She steadied it with her other hand and blinked hard, trying to gather herself. She glanced out at the yard, to the pale hydrangea bush Meredith had planted last spring, now starting to lose its color at the edges. Even that—the soft decay of petals— felt like too much.

The sunroom hummed with stillness. No music played. No phone buzzed. There was only the soft ticking of the little iron clock on the shelf and the low, familiar presence of a friend who had, for all her quirks, never once asked Claire to explain herself.

She breathed in, shallow and uneven, and stared at a spot on the windowpane where a single fingerprint had smudged the glass.

That night, after the girls were asleep and the house finally felt still enough to breathe, Claire found Mark in the living room staring at the television. The screen was dark. He wasn't watching anything.

The soft buzz of electricity gave the screen a faint, bluish sheen, just enough to cast a pale glow across his face. His expression was blank, distant—not contemplative, not burdened, just absent. The remote lay untouched on the cushion beside him. His hands rested on his knees. He hadn't noticed the lights dimming outside. He hadn't moved when the hallway clock chimed softly downstairs.

Claire stood behind the couch and said nothing.

She didn't cross her arms. She didn't speak his name. She didn't clear her throat to announce her presence. She let the silence stretch and settle, heavy as wool. She didn't need to make herself known—he already knew she was there. She felt it in the shift of his breath. The faint tightening of his shoulders.

The air in the room was stale with the scent of whatever had burned slightly on the stove earlier. The only light came from a table lamp dimmed so low it gave off the amber cast of candlelight. From where she stood, Claire could see the faint outline of one of Sadie's dolls, half-buried beneath the throw blanket, its plastic arm reaching out over the edge of the ottoman like a forgotten offering. A child's bracelet was on the floor nearby—tiny pink beads arranged in an uneven loop, a thread of innocence threaded through the stillness.

He spoke first. "I'm sorry."

It was so soft she almost didn't hear it.

The words didn't come with weight or performance. They weren't accompanied by a shift in posture or the glance of a man seeking forgiveness. He said it like a truth too tired to be resisted. A sentence that had lived in his throat long enough to wear grooves.

She walked around and sat beside him. Not touching. Not close. Just near.

She kept her body rigid but neutral, her hands clasped loosely in her lap, her gaze fixed on the television screen that glowed with silent nothing. The room seemed to hold its breath.

He didn't look at her.

His eyes were still forward, focused on the absence of image. His jaw twitched once, barely perceptible, and then went still again.

"I'm not seeing anyone," she said quietly.

Her voice was clear but stripped bare. The kind of sentence you speak when there's no room left for pretending. She didn't look at him as she said it. She didn't wait for affirmation.

"I know."

His response was immediate, low, unembellished. But he still didn't turn to face her.

A beat passed.

She listened to the small sounds of the house—the tick of the baseboard heater expanding as it cooled, the faint creak of the bannister upstairs settling into quiet. Her mind played tricks, imagining footsteps, whispers, the rustle of someone moving through the hallways. She blinked the thoughts away.

"I've just felt... distant," she said. "Like you've been disappearing in front of me."

The truth of it stung as it left her mouth. It sounded small when spoken aloud, compared to the way it had consumed her in private.

He exhaled. "I have. I know I have."

The words came out flat, exhausted. He ran a hand down his thigh but didn't move closer. Didn't lean in.

"Why?"

She said it gently, not like a demand. There was no accusation in her tone. Only a strange, weary curiosity, as if she were asking about a weather pattern neither of them could control.

He swallowed. His throat moved.

"I don't know," he said. "I think I... I think I'm ashamed."

That word sat in the space between them like a weight.

She looked at him then. Really looked. For the first time in weeks, maybe months, he seemed like a person. Not a wall.

His shoulders had slumped forward just slightly. The artificial blue light softened the lines of his face, making him look older than he was. The facade had cracked, not in a grand gesture, but in the subtle way the corners of his mouth downturned when he thought no one would notice.

"I love the girls," he added. "But sometimes I don't know how to be... this."

She nodded. "I know."

She didn't offer a solution. There was no quick answer. She only acknowledged the chasm, the absence, the truth. That was all she had left to offer.

He turned toward her. "Are we okay?"

Her heart broke a little more with the question.

It wasn't just the content of the question. It was the fact that he asked it with such simplicity, as if they were merely off course instead of unraveling at the seams. As if this were repairable.

She reached for his hand and held it loosely, like a ribbon slipping through fingers.

"I want us to be."

But even as the words left her mouth, a flicker of something darker twisted low in her chest—doubt, suspicion, survival. She wondered, fleetingly, if he was apologizing for the silence or the surveillance. If he was trying to close the distance… or cover a trail.

And wanting wasn't enough anymore. Wanting was a quiet ache. It did nothing against the presence of threat.

When she let go of his hand, it was careful, measured. She didn't draw back sharply. She simply allowed her fingers to fall away. The distance returned at once—subtle but absolute. He turned his face away again. The spell, if it ever was one, had passed.

Upstairs, the hallway light glowed beneath the girls' bedroom doors, a small rectangular beacon of the life she was still holding together with threadbare hands. She imagined their tiny legs tangled in blankets, their hair damp from rushed baths, their small breaths rising and falling in perfect, untroubled rhythm. They had no idea what it meant to feel this frayed. To feel like the walls were watching. Like the floorboards remembered things you thought you buried.

Claire stood slowly. Her legs ached—not from sitting but from everything. The unrelenting tension. The invisible armor she wore every day. The performative stillness that exhausted her more than movement ever could. Her body was tired of holding so much. She walked up the stairs one at a time, without touching the railing. Her fingertips hovered above the wall as she passed, brushing just close enough to feel the slight change in temperature where a vent blew warm air through.

After she went to the bed, sliding beneath the comforter without turning on the lamp, she lay with her eyes open for a long time.

She thought about Meredith. The soft encouragement in her voice. The way she poured wine without question. The kind of loyalty that looked like safety.

She thought about David. About the hallway. About what she'd seen.

And then she thought about what would happen next. What she would do if anyone came closer. What she was willing to become if forced.

The ceiling stared down in silence.

And Claire, who had spent so much time trying to earn peace through stillness, through sacrifice, through small acts of invisibility, finally understood that stillness wasn't the same as safety.

It was time to stop dissolving. It was time to reassemble. She blinked into the dark, one last thought coiling in the center of her mind:

If they come for me again, they won't find the same woman.

Chapter Fourteen

The Lake House

He hadn't meant to bring her here.

It was never supposed to be this place. Not this house with its old sun-bleached siding and dock that creaked like a memory you couldn't shake. It wasn't just about logistics, or secrecy, or convenience—those were the surface-level lies men told themselves when they wanted to believe they still had control. No, the lake house meant something else entirely. Something that used to be clean. Untouched.

This house had been a refuge once, a quiet reliquary from a better version of himself, preserved in pinewood and late August air. A place where he and Claire, still half-formed and overly hopeful, had fumbled through the first fragile iterations of togetherness, tasting a future they couldn't yet name—let alone survive.

Now it felt desecrated.
The scent of old summers clung to the curtains—sun lotion and wood smoke and mildewed towels that had dried stiff on the porch railings. There had been children's laughter here once. Late-night wine. Marshmallows melted into hair. Now, it all smelled like something left too long in the back of the fridge.

She stepped inside ahead of him, her arrival changing the molecular structure of the air. A breeze followed her in, chilled and faintly perfumed, like wind slipping through a cracked car window on a dangerous drive. Her heels struck the floorboards with unapologetic precision, the sound too sharp, too possessive—an intrusion carved into the ribs of the house itself.

Her coat slipped off her shoulders with a whisper of silk, catching briefly on the edge of her elbow before sliding free. There was nothing accidental in the gesture. Watching her undress was like watching someone dismantle a bomb in reverse—graceful, calculated, inevitable.

She scanned the room with a cool, cataloguing eye. Not fondness. Not nostalgia. Just quiet judgment.

"So this is where the perfect family spends its weekends." Mark dropped his bag beside the door. Too hard. The sound echoed, hollow and misplaced, like a shot fired in the wrong room. He clenched his jaw before speaking, trying to keep the bitterness from cracking open. "It's not like that."

"No?" She approached the fireplace, trailing one hand along the mantel with a surgeon's delicacy. Her fingertip drew a slow path through the dust, leaving a pale wound behind. "Then what is it like, Mark?"

He had no answer. Or rather, he had too many—all of them useless now. The question sat between them like a lit match, daring him to speak, to try to justify the unravelling story of his life. But he couldn't. Not anymore.

She found the liquor with the ease of someone used to crossing thresholds that weren't hers. No hesitation. No permission sought. The clink of the decanter, the low pour of amber liquid, the soft sigh of glass against lip—each sound pressed deeper into the silence until it rang like judgment.

She draped herself across the couch with feline confidence, curling into the cushions like she'd always belonged there. A woman who had long ago stopped waiting to be invited. She never asked—she simply was. And he watched her from the doorway, arms heavy, skin too tight over a body he no longer recognized as entirely his.

This woman—this thing with a name he never dared speak aloud near Claire—looked like a solution and a warning all at once.

The weight in his chest wasn't guilt.   Not exactly.

It was something heavier.

Something with roots.

Something that whispered: you were always going to do this. "You're thinking again," she murmured, her glass swirling like a pendulum. "Stop doing that." "I'm not—"

She cut him off with the laziest of smiles, the kind that said she already knew everything he hadn't said. "You're wondering what this makes you. A liar? A cheat? A husband in decline?"

"I didn't say that."
"You didn't have to." She crossed one leg over the other, lashes fluttering like closing doors. "You've been falling into other women's arms ever since you started noticing how Claire stacks up beside them. Don't look so shocked. I'm not offended. It's what men do. They compare. They recalibrate. They look at their wives folding laundry in the

196

same stretched-out pajamas they've worn since the Bush administration, and suddenly every passing waitress looks like salvation."

Mark laughed—once. A dry, splintered sound. Not humor. Not even protest. Just a crack in the veneer. "Jesus."

"Too close to home?"

He sank down beside her, not quite touching, as if distance might dilute the damage. The cushion gave slightly beneath him, warm from her body.

"I didn't bring you here to fight."

"Of course not." She took a long sip. "You brought me here because you're tired of pretending. And because it's easier to be a different man in a different zip code."

Her gaze stayed pinned to his. "Tell me I'm wrong."

Mark's eyes drifted to the fireplace—cold, unused, but still holding the scent of old woodsmoke. Claire hadn't been here in months, but she was everywhere. In the tidy rows of labeled pantry jars. In the little throw blanket folded over the arm of the chair. In the air itself, which still carried her lavender-and-laundry scent, ghostlike and unbearable.

"She's not the same," he said quietly. "Claire. She's changed."

"And what about you?" the woman asked, voice low and poisonous-sweet. "Still pure of heart?" He exhaled through his nose, laugh barely there. "Hardly."

"You want to believe you're a good man. A faithful husband forced into moral compromise by circumstance." She tilted her head. "But the truth is, your hands were already filthy before she ever looked away." His silence answered for him.

"She's paranoid," she said. "Erratic. She watches you like she's waiting for the blow to fall. Like she's already decided you're the monster in her story."   "I don't know if she's wrong."

"You're not dangerous, Mark," she said, and this time her smile softened enough to pass for compassion. "You're just scared. And scared men make messy choices."

He stood abruptly, the sudden motion jarring the table. The room felt too small, the ceiling lower than it had been a minute ago. Or maybe it was just the weight of her gaze pressing him into the floor.

"I've tried," he said. "I've really tried to make it work. For the girls."

"Oh, I know you have." She followed him slowly, never rushing, always measuring. "But Claire doesn't make it easy, does she? One minute she's crying, the next she's gone cold, and then she's looking at you like you're the one hiding something."

Mark spun around, voice rising. "She went to a hotel. She lied about it. I saw the charge."

"And have you asked yourself why?" she murmured, closer now. Her voice changed—low, rhythmic, intimate like a knife against skin. "Because she's hiding something. Something you're too afraid to name."

He said nothing.

"She's not just unhappy. She's unwell."

He scrubbed a hand down his face, feeling the grit of the day on his skin. "I don't know what to think anymore."

"I do." She took a step closer. "You once told me you took out a life insurance policy on her." His stomach twisted. "That was years ago."   "But it's still active."

"I didn't mean it like that."

"Didn't you?" she asked, tilting her head. "You said you were scared she'd hurt herself. Or someone else. That if anything ever happened, you had to be ready. That's not betrayal, Mark. That's what smart men call foresight."

He sat heavily on the couch, elbows on knees, hands locked behind his neck.

"She's unraveling," the woman said, circling slowly now. "You said so yourself. She's suspicious. Unpredictable. She's dragging your name into whatever dark thing she's hiding. What if she does something worse? What if she takes the girls down with her?"

"Stop."

But she didn't.

"What if she ruins you? All of it—your career, your reputation, your daughters' lives. What happens when she finally burns it all to the ground?"

"I'm not killing my wife," he whispered.

"No one said you were." She crouched in front of him now, hands on his knees, her voice velvet-wrapped steel. "But maybe it's time to consider your options. You're not a villain. You're just a man standing in the ashes of something that already died."

He looked up at her, eyes rimmed red, heart thudding like a fist against hollow wood. "You make it sound so simple." "It is," she whispered, and brushed her lips—soft, deliberate—against his cheek. "You just haven't admitted it yet."

Chapter Fifteen

The Setup

The house was empty for the first time in what felt like a lifetime. Not quiet — it had not been truly quiet in months, not since the first shadow of doubt unfurled across the marriage bed — but empty in a way that seemed unnatural, almost theatrical, as though the silence had been staged. The walls no longer vibrated with the chaos of children or the tension of withheld glances across the breakfast table. There was only stillness now, thick and watchful, as though the house itself were holding its breath, waiting for something it didn't want to see.

The girls were gone. Emma at Ava's for a weekend sleepover involving movie marathons and lip gloss; Sadie at Grace's, likely already in pajamas and asking for extra syrup on her waffles. Two different homes. Two zip codes. Two safe, parent-vetted destinations Claire had secured with the smooth efficiency of a woman who had once brokered secrets over champagne without blinking.

She had made it seem casual — a surprise treat for her girls — but in truth, it had been orchestrated like an escape plan.

A smile as she zipped their backpacks. A kiss on each head as they bounded into other people's cars. Then the door had closed, and she was alone in the house with the weight of her own knowing.

She didn't move for a long time. Just stood with her back to the door, one hand still resting on the handle, as if she wasn't entirely sure whether to bolt it shut or wrench it open. Her lungs refused to expand fully. Her chest felt tight, the way it sometimes did in crowded rooms when she hadn't yet identified the threat but could feel it pulsing beneath the surface. It was a familiar sensation now. Her body had learned to anticipate betrayal before her mind allowed it language.

Mark was in "New York." That was the fiction. A business trip, allegedly, involving a pitch presentation uptown and drinks with a client whose name kept changing. She hadn't questioned it aloud — not in the old, direct way. That had stopped months ago. What she did instead was watch. Watch the way he packed, fast and loose, with none of the absentminded tenderness of a man who might miss the person he was leaving behind. Watch how he folded clothes like props, how he stood too long in front of the mirror adjusting a shirt collar that wouldn't lay flat. He had smiled at her like a bad actor remembering his lines too late. No kiss. No eye contact that lasted. No request to water the plants or pick up the dry cleaning. Just the jangle of his keys and the closing of the door behind him.

But it was the calendar that betrayed him.
She had seen it that morning, a hastily renamed entry on their shared app: **Lake View Conference**. Not a real event. Just two words meant to look innocuous. Except they

weren't. Not to her. Not when *Lake View* was what they used to call it — the lake house, the retreat, the place they once swore would be a permanent escape from the ordinary. Before it all curdled. Before the silence between them grew long and brittle and hungry. Lake View was their euphemism. And now he was using it again, as if it still meant the same thing, as if it hadn't been repurposed for a lie.

She didn't hesitate. Not anymore.

Claire moved like she was answering an alarm only she could hear. She packed nothing sentimental. No notes. No goodbye letters. No relics of who she had once tried to be. Just a clean change of clothes. A flashlight. And a kitchen knife that slid into the lining of her bag like it had always belonged there. She didn't need to bring proof — she carried it in her bloodstream. The evidence no longer lived in drawers or boxes. It lived in memory. In muscle. In her dreams and her shadows.

The drive out was long and pulseless. She didn't turn on the radio. She didn't let herself rehearse what she would say if she caught them. Words were futile things now — too small for the size of her rage, too civilized for what she feared she might become. The sky was a deepening bruise as she left the city, a slow collapse of light that felt both cosmic and personal. The road narrowed.

The trees thickened. Her phone buzzed once — a calendar reminder she didn't check — and then she powered it off and left it in the glove compartment.

She parked half a mile from the lake house, just past the old split-rail fence, where the gravel gave way to pine needles and shadows. The forest was impossibly quiet, the kind of silence that made you feel like you were already being watched. She walked the rest of the way on foot, the soles of her boots nearly soundless on the moss and stone. Her breath moved like fog in the cold air, rising and dissolving before it reached eye level.

She saw it before she felt it.

The lake house.

Nestled beneath overgrown trees, the porch swing hanging crooked, the curtains drawn against the evening, like eyelids closed over a secret. The lights were on. Warm. Intentional. Through the slits in the living room she could see movement — a hand reaching for a wine glass, the flicker of a shadow that wasn't Mark's. Her heart contracted so hard she almost staggered.

His car was in the drive. Parked with careless ease, like he had no reason to hide.

Claire didn't go to the front door. She crept around the back, where the kitchen window glowed against the darkness like a stage light. She crouched low and watched, the way you might watch
a house you once lived in after the fire — marveling at the ruin, stunned by how much still stood. Inside, she saw his shape. Mark. Leaning against the counter. Shirt unbuttoned. Laughing at something.

And then — *her*.
A woman's arm. A delicate hand with a wine glass. The unmistakable gleam of red curls under soft lighting. The scent of something expensive wafted out through the slightly ajar window. Claire's throat closed around it. A scent she had smelled before. On coat collars. In the car. Once,

204

clinging to the scarf of her youngest daughter after a school drop-off.

Claire didn't cry. She didn't scream. She didn't fall to her knees or collapse into the bushes or shake with the shock of it all.

She simply *knew*.

Knew it the way you know when a storm is coming by the feel of the pressure behind your eyes. Knew it the way a dog knows to run before the ground shakes. There had never been any innocence in Meredith. Just the performance of it — smooth and soft and practiced. She had inserted herself with surgical precision, always knowing exactly what to say, how to console, when to call.

Claire moved for the back door.

She still had the key. Not because she believed in nostalgia, but because she never discarded tools. The lock turned without resistance, the old click of it oddly tender in the dark. She stepped inside.

The scent hit her first — red wine and perfume and something sweeter. Strawberries, maybe. The overhead light was soft, casting long shadows across the floor. Music played faintly from a speaker in the other room — something low and jazzy, the kind of music chosen by people pretending not to be afraid of silence.

She heard footsteps on the stairs. She ducked behind the coat closet, every muscle taut and alert. Then a voice — not Mark's.

A voice she recognized from somewhere deeper, older.

"You're early."

Claire turned slowly, the air congealing around her like tar.

He stood at the top of the stairs. Jeff. The stranger from the grocery store. The man from Room 604. The voice on the radio. No uniform now. No mask. Just the kind of calm that made her blood ice.
"You're not as careful as you think you are, Delia."

That name.
That name that wasn't a name but a version of herself built from necessity and survival and shame. Hearing it aloud was like being slapped across a decade.
He moved down the stairs with surgical precision.

"I watched you bury it all under PTA meetings and perfect teeth," he said. "But rot always rises. And you were always going to end up back here. Like gravity."
Claire backed into the dresser. Her fingers reached for the drawer out of instinct, remembering a time when she used to keep a weapon there.

Jeff smiled. "Mark's not the one pulling strings. He's just a confused little boy playing with matches." Her breath caught. "You've been watching us." He nodded, slow and solemn. "I've been *in* your house." His voice was a scalpel.

"Cameras. Motion sensors. Audio. You really should've changed your locks after the first warning."

She lunged. He grabbed her wrist mid-air, slamming her back into the dresser hard enough to shake the lamp. Her head struck wood. Stars burst across her vision. "I should've finished it a year ago," he hissed. "Room 604 was supposed to be your end." "You killed David," she gasped.

"And you were supposed to go next," he said simply. "But you always did know how to run." He reached for something in his belt — a flash of silver.
But Claire twisted, used her weight, and kicked hard — both legs. He stumbled. She broke free, bolted down the stairs, heart pounding like a war drum in her throat.
She grabbed the cast iron skillet from the stove — the heaviest thing in reach — and turned just as he reached the last step.
She swung.

The sound it made was something ancient.

He collapsed.

His badge rolled across the floor and disappeared beneath the counter. His body landed in a sprawl, eyes open but unseeing, neck at a terrible angle.

Claire didn't check for a pulse.
She walked to the door, hand trembling, skin slick with sweat and fear.
And there they were.

Mark.

And *her*.
Red curls. Black coat. A lipstick shade Claire had never worn, but had seen many times — on napkins, glasses, collars.

Meredith.

Chapter Sixteen

The Saint

There had been a time—long before her name became synonymous with rot and calculation, long before the blood pooled beneath a man she once pretended to love, and long before vengeance began to stretch itself like sinew through the quiet hollows of her body—when Meredith could still sing. Not just passably. Not merely well. But beautifully, hauntingly, with a kind of aching precision that silenced entire rooms and, for a moment, made even the worst men believe in grace.

It was never effortless, even in the beginning, but back then the strain had been exhilarating—like standing on the edge of a rooftop in heels and knowing exactly how long you could balance there before the wind turned mean. She had studied breath the way other girls studied boys—how to harness it, discipline it, control it until it lived low in her body and bloomed on command. Her shoulders were trained to stay relaxed, her face an instrument she sculpted nightly into invitation, her gaze softened just enough to make strangers trust her, though she never returned the favor.

At Juilliard, where dreams collided with exhaustion and genius often looked like madness, Meredith learned not just how to sing but how to hold suffering in her mouth without letting it distort her face. They had taught her that vulnerability, when packaged correctly, could pass for artistry—and that women, especially women who wanted to be adored, needed to bleed beautifully or not at all.

She remembered the rooms—dim, smoky places that smelled like old bourbon and velvet and the kind of regrets men paid to drown in. She remembered how the lights pressed against her skin like hands, how the piano's lid gleamed like a lake at night, and how the hush always fell just before the music started, that sacred silence laced not with reverence but anticipation, the room collectively leaning forward to hear what would be taken from her next.

Her voice had once curled through the air like steam from a cup of something forbidden, gliding past upturned collars and carefully crossed legs, brushing the backs of necks and lingering at the rims of glasses. It didn't seduce—it ensnared. It made people ache without knowing why. It gave form to feelings they could not name.

She was never famous, not in the way some women were: no marquee spelled her name in lights, no records lined the shelves of lonely men, no interviews were clipped and saved. But in certain circles—dark, red-lit corners filled with old money and older appetites—her name was whispered like a secret that might ruin you if spoken too loudly.

Then came David.

He did not arrive with charm, or flowers, or feigned humility. He did not flatter, or flirt, or place his hand on the small of her back like he believed in destiny. He was not seductive in any traditional sense. But he had that other thing—that dense, unsmiling gravity that men of great wealth develop when they no longer bother explaining themselves.

He moved like someone who had never once needed to raise his voice to get what he wanted. He didn't ask for attention; he expected it. He didn't compliment her gown or her voice or her mind. He simply looked at her like she had already been acquired, and in doing so, she became his.

He liked Meredith in red—true red, the kind that couldn't be softened by candlelight or mistaken for wine. He liked her quiet—not silenced, exactly, but disciplined, reserved, hollowed out. He liked her folded beside him like a silk handkerchief, the kind tucked into the breast pocket of a man who wanted to suggest elegance without saying a word.

So she gave him what he wanted.

She wore red.

She wore silence.

She shaved off the sharper parts of herself, trimmed the edges of her voice until it curved only around him, and taught her body to lean at the right angle, her smile to hold just long enough, her thoughts to retreat like water down a drain.
And when he died—alone in a hotel suite whose carpet would never come clean again, blood spreading slowly around him like a forgotten promise—he left her everything. The accounts. The assets. The houses with too many rooms

and not enough memories. But he also left her something more corrosive.

A name.

Claire Holloway.

It was tucked away, not hidden exactly, but folded into the folds of his digital life like something he'd meant to deal with and never did. It lived in his phone—between dinner receipts and travel itineraries and a half-drafted email that began with *I know I've failed you*. Meredith had opened it without surprise, without flinching, without blinking. She stared at the name, that single fragile syllable, for a long time—long enough for the silence to thicken, for the air to shift, for the shape of the world to begin quietly rearranging itself around her.
She did not cry. She did not scream or slam a drawer or stumble dramatically across the kitchen floor. She did not whisper the name aloud. She did not say it at all.

Instead, she reached for her phone, and she called Jeff.

Her brother had always been the thing behind the thing. Where Meredith was velvet and wine and music, Jeff was concrete and wire and blood. He wore suits now, expensive ones, and he knew how to smile when the situation demanded it, but the violence inside him had never gone dormant.
He had been her protector since they were children—since the night their father dragged their mother by the hair through the kitchen for daring to sing over the sound of the news, since Meredith had stood frozen, and Jeff had picked up a lamp and thrown it.

He didn't talk about it. But he never forgot it.

He didn't believe in forgiveness. He believed in family.

"She was with him," Meredith said, her voice a slow knife. "At the hotel. I want them both gone."

He didn't ask questions. He never had.

But Claire—whoever she truly was—was already gone. She had slipped the scene, vanished before Jeff could complete whatever quiet resolution he'd planned. Whether he froze, or faltered, or failed, Meredith never knew. He never offered the full account, and she never asked for it.

All she received was a single text, unceremonious and flat: *David's dead. But she's alive.* That was all.
She had stared at those words until they blurred, until they bled into one another, until her reflection on the screen stared back hollow-eyed and bright with something ancient.

She could have ruined Claire with one well-timed whisper.

Could have exposed her, hunted her, torn the fabric of her new life with a flick of her finger.
But that would have been messy. That would have been loud.

That would have been mercy.
Meredith didn't want chaos. She wanted collapse.

She wanted erosion.
She wanted a woman to watch everything she had built rot from the inside, not knowing where it began or when it might end.

So she waited.

She traced Claire's name.

Found the new address, the new life, the daughters with perfect hair and the husband who seemed present only when the lighting was good.

She watched the seasonal wreaths rotate on the front door like clockwork.

She attended school functions, mingled with mothers who mistook her smile for sincerity, and slowly drew a perfect little circle around Claire's carefully curated existence.

And then she stepped inside it.

She brought cookies. She brought stories. She brought softness wrapped in silk and handed it over like a gift. She became the friend—the confidante—the woman Claire whispered to when the cracks began to show.   And when the timing felt right—when Claire finally had something to lose—Meredith began to take.

First the cup, rinsed and dried but still faintly stained. Then the key card. Then the photos and the matchbook. She loved the game.
Each item moved with precision. Each item pulsing with doubt.
Jeff installed the cameras, timed the static in the kitchen radio, whispered threats through silence until Claire no longer trusted her own mind.
He played Detective Hollis like a part he'd always known was waiting for him. But even then, Meredith could feel something slipping.

Jeff began to hesitate.

There was something in his voice—some unspoken reluctance, some crack in the armor she didn't like.

So she turned to Mark.

Mark, who had been waiting for someone to tell him his unhappiness wasn't his fault. Mark, who still wanted to believe that good husbands strayed only when provoked.

She leaned into him like heat. She softened when he needed softness, hardened when he needed guilt.

And when he confessed the existence of the life insurance policy—the one he'd taken out years ago during a financial high—she smiled, but not too widely.
"You really think she'd do the same for you?" she asked, her voice like smoke curling against his neck.

He didn't answer.

He didn't need to.

She believed she had thought of everything.

Until Claire showed up at the lake house.

Chapter Seventeen

The Truth

The storm had begun only minutes earlier—rain slashing sideways across the wide lake house windows, thunder rolling in from the east like a slow-moving threat still deciding where to strike. It crept through the trees and funneled down the narrow gravel drive, churning up pine needles and fallen twigs until it reached the porch steps and climbed the walls of the house like it meant to stay.

Claire was already inside.
She stood in the living room without speaking, without moving, her body still and alert, as though she were part of the architecture now—fixed in place like a figure carved into the molding. The overhead light had been turned off. Only one lamp glowed in the far corner, its amber light struggling against the storm shadows that shifted like slow smoke across the floor. The air carried the scent of damp cedar and old lake water, tinged faintly with something coppery and wrong.

In the center of the room, slouched at an unnatural angle on the leather couch, Jeff bled onto a floral throw pillow that

now looked violently out of place. His wrists were zip-tied, one eye already swollen shut, blood drying in a rough crescent along his temple. His breathing was uneven but steady—shallow rises of the chest that confirmed what Claire already knew: he was still conscious.
Still with her. Still hers.

She hadn't needed to look at him in over twenty minutes. Her focus was on the French doors, slick with water, their panes shivering under the force of the wind. And then, at last, the shapes emerged—blurred silhouettes pressing through the storm, laughing low and close as they stepped onto the threshold like lovers slipping in from the world.

Meredith entered first, curls soaked and tangled, clinging to her skin in frizzed ropes. She moved with easy familiarity, her arms wrapped loosely around herself for warmth, her face lit with the kind of lazy smile that comes after wine or secrets. Her mascara had begun to run, drifting down her cheeks in soft gray trails that might have been tears if Claire didn't know better.

Mark followed just behind, his jacket unzipped, shoes wet, hair tousled from the wind. He looked relaxed, almost casual, his mouth curled into that vaguely amused smirk he wore like armor. There was something familiar in the way they moved together—a rhythm built from too many quiet moments no one had seen.

They were laughing softly.
That intimate kind of laughter that slips between people who think they're alone. The kind that's warmer than it should be.

The kind that doesn't belong in a room like this.
And then they saw him.
Jeff.

Meredith's smile disintegrated in an instant. Her expression collapsed like a paper cup crushed in a fist. Her hand flew to her mouth, her eyes widening with such pure shock Claire almost believed it.

"Oh my God—Jeff?"
Her voice cracked. She rushed forward, instinct overruling everything, panic flaring like heat. But Mark was faster. His arms wrapped tightly around her waist, holding her back—not like a protector, but like someone stopping a trap from springing too early.
"Don't," he said, his tone steady and cool. "Claire's here."

Meredith froze in his grasp. Her eyes snapped toward the far side of the room. And there, in the edge of the lamplight, Claire stepped forward like a figure emerging from smoke. "Hello, Meredith," she said, her voice quiet, flat, not needing to be loud. The storm answered for her—a burst of thunder crashing through the walls and floors like a second heartbeat. "What is this?" Meredith asked, her voice rising higher, sharp with disbelief.
"Why is he tied up? What—what the hell did you do?"
"She tried to kill him!" Meredith shouted, struggling violently against Mark's arms now. "Let me go—" Claire didn't move. She didn't blink. "If I wanted him dead," she said clearly, "he'd be dead."Jeff groaned. It was a low, guttural sound, a rasp of protest or pain or both. He shifted on the couch, testing his bonds, wincing as the plastic pulled tighter against torn skin. Blood trickled slowly down the

curve of his jaw, painting a fresh line through the bruises already blooming there.

Meredith's chest heaved, breath coming fast, hands balled into fists. "You're insane."

Claire tilted her head, eyes steady. "Not insane," she said. "Just… tired of being polite."

Mark loosened his hold on Meredith with deliberate slowness, his hands falling away like a stage cue. She stumbled forward one step, as if unsure of her own footing, then froze again when she saw how still Jeff was.

Claire didn't move. "Do you want to help him?" she asked. "Or do you want to finish what you started?"

Meredith blinked rapidly. "What?"

"You sent him, didn't you?" Claire asked. "The night David died. You told
Jeff to handle it."

"That's not true—"

"But it is," Claire said, cutting her off before the lie could land. "You told your brother here—Detective Hollis—to teach him a lesson. Maybe take care of the girl, too."

Meredith's mouth opened. Nothing came out. Her throat worked but no sound emerged.

"I wasn't in the room when he died," Claire continued. Her voice was steady now. Slower. Heavier. "I left. Took a call. When I came back… David was on the floor. Bleeding. Still breathing, but fading fast."

She paused. "I took the money and left."

Jeff stirred at that—let out a sharp, wounded exhale through his nose that was half anger, half disbelief. Meredith flinched.

Claire turned her head slowly, gaze landing on him with surgical precision.

"That's right, isn't it, Jeff?" Then she moved.

She crossed the room in three quiet, perfect steps. Her boots didn't make a sound on the floorboards. She lowered herself in front of him with eerie control, knees bending until her eyes were level with his."You ruined so many lives," she said, and her voice was almost tender. "You hid in the shadows, called yourself a middleman. But you were just another predator. A coward."

Jeff coughed, and it sounded wet. He bared his teeth in something like a sneer. "You don't know what you're talking about."

"She knows exactly what she's talking about," Mark said, stepping out from the darkened hallway, his voice no longer masked with boredom.

Meredith's body snapped around toward him. "What?" Mark moved toward Claire, closing the space between them with slow, even steps. Not rushing. Not afraid. He didn't even look at Jeff.

"You're with her?" Meredith said, voice barely above a whisper now.

"You've been working with her?"

Mark looked at Claire first—just for a moment—and then back at Meredith with all the ease of someone finally telling the truth.

"Of course I am," he said, soft but final. "She's my wife." Meredith took a single step backward, like the air had been punched out of her.

"You've been playing me?"

Mark shrugged—just the faintest lift of one shoulder. "You weren't that hard to play."

The silence that followed wasn't empty. It was crowded—
with memory, suspicion, the slow crumbling of every
assumption.

Then Mark turned his head toward Claire again, and the
words came like a blade sliding free:

"Nice job, honey. Your acting skills are better than ever."

Claire didn't flinch. Didn't blink.

For the first time in weeks, her lips curled—slow and
certain.

"We're a great team."

Chapter Eighteen

The Recruit
Claire

The rain stopped just before sunrise. I could hear the wind moving through the trees again, not wild anymore, but slower, like it had tired itself out and was now folding back into the forest it came from.

I stood barefoot on the cold kitchen tiles, staring through the window above the sink. Outside, the lake stretched long and flat and dark, its surface like oil—no ripples, no wind, just the reflection of the heavy clouds still lingering overhead. The world looked paused, like it was waiting to see what I'd do next.

Jeff was no longer bleeding onto the couch. We'd dragged him downstairs hours ago—his body slumped, still semiconscious, zip-tied and groaning.
Now he was upright, lashed to a support beam in the basement, with a blanket beneath him and a damp rag pressed to his head. We weren't monsters. We were just done pretending.
Meredith was locked in the linen closet off the hallway. No windows. No handles on the inside. A tight little tomb of towels and cleaning products and her own shame. She'd

screamed for a while—guttural, high-pitched, pathetic. Then she started sobbing. And eventually she went still, like something inside her had collapsed in on itself.

Mark hadn't said much since we stepped out of character. There was nothing left to say. Years of strategy, whispers, surveillance, silence, restraint—and it had all led to this: a single night in the house where we could be alone, away from the girls. The performance was over. The audience was gone. The curtain had dropped. And we were still standing. I touched the edge of the countertop with my fingertips. The laminate was cool, smooth, strangely grounding. I stared at my reflection in the dark window—only partially visible, just a faint silhouette cast by the soft glow of the overhead pendant light. I looked like someone who'd come home from a war, but left half her soul behind.

And yet, I was more myself than I had ever been. Twelve years ago, I was twenty-two and invisible. I lived in a peeling one- room apartment above a pawn shop that smelled like burnt plastic and vinegar. The ceiling leaked. The floor stuck. My mattress sat on the ground next to a milk crate I used as a nightstand. I had four dollars left in my bank account and a head full of plans that would never come true.

I was smart. Hardened. Starving, both literally and metaphorically. I didn't believe in luck.
And I definitely didn't believe in help.
So when help arrived, it looked like something else entirely.
She approached me in a bookstore. That's the part that always feels surreal when I think back—like some storybook origin myth that couldn't possibly be real. She wore a long

camel coat, carried no bag, and had the kind of expression that made you feel like she already knew you. She complimented my boots. Asked if I worked nearby. Said I looked like someone with potential.

I remember the way she handed me the card—casual, but not careless. It was white and thick and unbranded. Just a number and a phrase printed in serif black:
Private Consultation. High-End Personal Strategy.
I stared at it for a day before I called.
Of course, I didn't know it then—but Jeff had sent her.

He never introduced himself. Never met me in person. Never even spoke to me directly until years later. At the time, he operated through a revolving door of intermediaries— always women, always elegant, always unreadable. They wore gray pencil skirts and matte lipstick. They called me sweetheart, but never smiled with their eyes.   They promised I'd be safe. That I'd be invisible. That I'd make more money in one week than I had seen in a year. They told me I could pick my own clothes, my own clients, my own hours. That no one would touch me unless I said yes. That nothing was expected—except professionalism. They lied.

That's how Delia was born.
She was expensive, she was professional. She never gave the same story twice. She wore heels taller than her fear and moved like someone who'd been trained to be forgotten. I became her so gradually I didn't even notice I'd stopped being me.Jeff kept his hands clean. He hid behind shell accounts and encrypted messaging apps and courier drop boxes. But he was always there.

Watching. Tracking. Profiting.

He wasn't a man back then—he was a presence. A threat disguised as a safety net.
The work was simple. I made men feel powerful. I kept them talking. I made them think they were dominant, that they were in control, that I was just another beautiful girl with no spine and fewer boundaries.
And yes, sometimes I slept with them.
Not always. But often enough to know what it cost. I didn't feel shame. I didn't cry afterward. I didn't break. I calculated.

They thought they were buying my body, but what they were really buying was the illusion of power. And I gave it to them—generously. I fed their egos. I nodded at their lies. I let them think they were gods. Because that's when they got sloppy. That's when they bragged. That's when they confessed.
I used their arrogance like a scalpel.
Some gave me leverage. Some gave me names. Some gave me silence.
And some gave me reasons.

I was never afraid of them. I was studying them. But over time, the work changed me. Not inside—I didn't lose my heart. I lost something deeper. My ability to feel disgusted. My ability to feel at all.
It wasn't about shame. It was about saturation.

My skin started to reject certain fabrics. I began to gag at the smell of hotel soap. I lost the ability to fall asleep unless there was noise in the hallway. My body was still mine—but only just.

I told Jeff I wanted out early on.

That's when things shifted.

The clients changed. Became rougher. Hungrier. The jobs got sloppier. Less luxury, more risk. I started getting bookings that weren't cleared through the usual channels. One day, I found a pair of my own underwear folded and placed neatly in my mailbox. That was the message: We see you. You belong to us.

But Jeff had never shown his face. Not once.

And I couldn't fight a ghost.

Then came the hotel room in D.C.

I was told it would be a standard client. High-ranking. Private. Discreet. Cash up front. My handler texted me the room number. I wore black.

When I opened the door, he was already there—sitting in a chair by the minibar, jacket still on, hands resting loosely on his knees.

He didn't stand. He didn't smile. He didn't even look impressed.

"Your name isn't Delia," he said.

I didn't respond.

"You're smarter than this," he said. "But you're being watched."

That was the first time I met Mark.

He wasn't a client. He was black ops—deep surveillance, long-term infiltration, domestic trafficking cases buried by politicians and money. He had been tracking one of my clients. Following a chain that led to corporate laundering,

private security firms, offshore accounts. And all of it—
every path—led to Jeff.

Mark didn't want what the others did. He wanted the truth.
And for some reason, I gave it to him.

He didn't report me. He didn't pity me. He offered me
something I hadn't seen in years—an exit.   He said,
"You're not broken. You're not ruined. You're
underutilized."

He trained me. Slowly at first. Then all at once. How to use
my intelligence like a knife. How to disappear inside a room.
How to make people underestimate me, and how to use that
underestimation like a weapon. How to disappear—and how
to be found when I wanted to be.

We got married a year later.

Not for cover. Not for optics. Because he knew who I was,
and he never looked away.

We built a life. Had children. Built walls. Played house while
gathering data.

We spent years trying to flush Jeff out. But every time we
got close, he disappeared again.

Until David.

A new name. A new client. A booking made through old
channels but flagged by newer protocols.

David Holbrook. A man Jeff didn't recognize. Not at first.
He had changed his name.

But once Jeff found out who David really was… it was too
late. His own brother-in-law. Meredith's husband. And he
had booked me.

That was the crack in the system. That was the breach we
needed.And just like that, everything began to fall apart—
right on schedule.

The rest… you already know.

I turned from the window. The light was different now—gray and diffused, the kind of colorless morning that leaves no shadows.

Mark stood at the top of the basement stairs, one hand braced on the doorframe. "We waited twelve years for this," he said. I nodded.
"We don't rush the ending," I said. "We make it count."

Chapter Nineteen

The Fall
Meredith

They weren't supposed to win.

Not because I thought they were incapable. Not because I underestimated Claire's intelligence or Mark's potential for cruelty. But because I had counted the pieces. I had watched them move across the board for over a year, and every move they made looked desperate. Scattershot. Reactive. I'd been sure they were behind the curve.

But now, sitting in the same room as them with the storm light drained from the windows and the air cold with aftermath, I realized they had never been behind.

They had been circling.

Claire was near the window, standing in a patch of early gray light. She wasn't facing me. She hadn't looked at me since the screaming stopped. Her profile was still, severe.

Arms crossed loosely, not in defense—but in control.

Like she had nothing more to brace against.

Across the room, Jeff sat slumped in the corner chair, wrists bound to the wooden arms with reinforced zip ties. His breathing was shallow now, uneven, but steady enough to remind me he wasn't gone yet. His shirt was soaked through with old blood, his head tilted at a strange angle, one eye nearly swollen shut. I could barely recognize him anymore. Mark stood by the door with the posture of someone not worried about what would happen next—because he already knew. He hadn't spoken in the last twenty minutes. Not to Claire. Not to me. Not even to Jeff. Just silence, deliberate and watchful.

I was the only one trembling.

"You set me up," I said, my voice raw from the last hour, stripped of performance. It wasn't a question. It wasn't even an accusation. Just the final flicker of disbelief clinging to what remained of my dignity.

Claire didn't flinch. Didn't answer. Didn't even tilt her head to acknowledge me.

I turned to Jeff. His eye flicked toward me for half a second. Blank. Fading. I hated the way he looked—small. Useless. He was supposed to be the cleanup.
The shield. The hand that reached into the fire while I stayed untouched.
"Say something," I rasped. "Tell them it wasn't all me." Still nothing.
I tried to move forward—just one step—but my legs betrayed me. My right knee buckled slightly and before I could fall, Mark's arm came out, firm and mechanical, pressing against my shoulder like a gate that would not budge.
"Don't," he said. Just that. Quiet. Final.
I stopped.

The rug beneath me had a winding, floral pattern, but from above, it looked like a snarl of veins—blue, strangling, suffocating the floor. The air had taken on that heavy, metallic stillness that only happens after something irreversible.

"I didn't mean for it to go this far," I whispered, voice cracking as the edges of the lie frayed.

Claire turned, slowly this time, eyes settling on me with the steadiness of a blade before it drops.

"You mean," she said evenly, "it wasn't supposed to end with you in the wrong room."

The words landed so softly they might have floated—but they hit like stone.

"I only wanted to scare her," I said. It sounded thin. Pathetic. Embarrassed, even to me.

"No," she said. "You wanted to dismantle me."

I shook my head. "I wanted answers."

"No," Claire said again, sharper this time. "You wanted punishment."

She took a step toward the center of the room, her movements smooth and eerily slow, like someone walking through water. She wasn't trying to intimidate. "You found my name on David's phone," she said, voice lower now, more intimate. "That's how it started."

I swallowed hard. "He was my husband."

Claire's face didn't move. "He was a predator." I said nothing.

"He booked me under a false name. Bypassed protocol. Your husband has been abusive to most of the other ladies, he'd stolen my ID from my bag on a previous booking. He was a predatory asshole.

Claire's voice didn't crack. If anything, it got steadier. "He threatened me," she said. "Tried to control me. Humiliate me. He thought he owned me just because he paid." I felt something tighten in my chest. "Before I left to take a call, your husband pushed me up against a wall, put

his hand over my neck and told me if I wouldn't do what he wanted he would take what he wanted anyway. He said it wouldn't be the first time. I got out, took a call, took a breath, and when I came back, he was on the floor bleeding. Still breathing. But alone. I didn't help him. I didn't care if he lived.

And then… I took the money and walked away." She turned slightly, just enough to glance at Jeff.

"You sent him to finish it, to finish me…but that was never going to happen."

I opened my mouth to protest, but Mark stepped closer now. I could feel the energy shift—like the next domino had just been tapped.

"We have your voice," he said.

I frowned. "What?"

Claire reached into her coat pocket and pulled out a small black recorder. She pressed a button. Static. Then my voice, too clear to deny.

"He's at the Mason Hill Suites. Room 604. Take care of it. And her."

I closed my eyes. I remembered leaving that voicemail. I remembered thinking I was being careful, using the right phrasing. Cold, professional.

Detached.

I hadn't been careful enough.

"You tricked me," I breathed. "That's entrapment."

"No," Claire said, slipping the recorder back into her pocket.

"That's a confession."

I staggered back again, felt the edge of the wall catch my shoulder.

Jeff made a small, rasping sound in his chair. It might have been a cough. It might have been his last breath.

Mark knelt down beside him and checked his pulse. Claire didn't move. She watched Mark the way someone watches a fire burn out.

"He's gone," Mark said after a long moment.

The words were almost casual.

He stood, pulled out his phone.

"Patch me to Kingbird," he said quietly, like ordering takeout.

My blood ran cold.

Claire stepped beside him. Their shoulders barely touched, but the unity between them felt unbreakable.

The phone clicked.

"It's done," Mark said.

He ended the call and slid the phone back into his coat without looking at me.My breath caught. "What is this? Who are you people?"

Claire turned to me, and for the first time all morning, I saw something flicker behind her eyes—not anger. Not joy.

Just purpose.

"You'll be prosecuted formally," she said. "The evidence has already been submitted. Obstruction. Conspiracy.

Attempted murder. And more."

I laughed once. Sharp. Stupid. "You think a judge is going to believe you over me?"

She blinked, slowly. "I don't need belief. I have proof." I looked at Jeff again, as if some part of him might rise up and undo this.

But he was slumped now. Completely still.

Claire and Mark didn't gloat. They didn't posture. They just stood there as I came undone.

And I realized, with a sickening weight in my gut, that they hadn't out played me. They'd out waited me.

They'd known exactly what I'd do.

And they had let me do it.

Chapter Twenty

The Wife
Claire

The evening folded in on itself like the slow, inevitable end of a storm—one that didn't vanish but hung in the sky with a kind of bruised warning, quiet but charged. The rain had passed hours ago, leaving the windows streaked and fogged, the scent of wet pine rising through the vents. The lake beyond the trees shimmered in a dark, metallic blue, its surface flat as glass, as if daring someone to test its stillness. In the quietest corner of the kitchen, a soft hum echoed from the refrigerator, the only sound in a house that now knew everything.

Mark stood near the counter, one hand braced casually on the marble edge, the other curled around a glass he hadn't yet filled. His eyes followed me without speaking, not out of suspicion. He watched me the way a soldier studies a weapon he's used in battle—familiar, lethal, and marked with something deeper than fear: respect. He didn't smile. But something in the angle of his jaw, the steady rhythm of his breath, the ease with which he met my gaze—told me everything I needed to know. We were aligned again, not as man and wife, not even as friends, but as co-architects of something that would outlive both of us.

He finally moved—slow and deliberate—filling a glass with water and handing it to me. It wasn't affection. It wasn't habit. It was acknowledgment, quiet and direct, the kind of ritual you don't need to speak about once you've bled together.

Our fingers brushed. My pulse didn't change. Neither did his. I drank deeply, let the cold water pull me back into my body. It was over. The hardest part. The part where someone had to die.
And Jeff had died.

We didn't speak of it, but his body had already been handled, the call already made, the evidence already neutralized. Mark had taken care of the iron skillet. I'd cleaned the upholstery. He'd mopped the floor with quiet, mechanical efficiency. We didn't flinch. We never had. Because this wasn't panic. It was protocol.I moved to the far end of the kitchen, to the cabinet with the deep, drawer-less base. From the outside, it looked like a decorative panel, just another flourish in a well-designed home. But inside— behind a smooth magnetic seal—was our safe. Seamless. Cold. Invisible to anyone who didn't already know it was there.

I knelt, tapped the pressure latch in the lower right corner, and pressed my thumb to the print reader hidden just beneath the lip. The panel hissed open.
Inside sat a burner phone, its matte black screen dark and waiting. Next to it lay a laminated contact card, two encrypted flash drives, a slim pack of surgical gloves, a single-gun holster with no weapon in it, and a yellow manila folder sealed with a plain black clip.

I took the phone and powered it on. No password required. It never had one. The number was memorized. I dialed. The line didn't ring. It never rang. Just a click. A breath. The faint hum of someone else waiting in a darker room. "Confirmed," I said. My voice didn't quiver. It never had. I ended the call and returned the phone exactly where I'd found it, aligning it with the edge of the box inside the safe. I picked up the folder and laid it on the counter before closing the safe, sealing it again with a quiet magnetic lock. The cabinet looked like nothing had ever happened. Mark was still watching me. But now, he smiled. That rare, slow, knowing smile. The one he used to give me before a mission, before a kiss, before a kill.
I smiled back—wider.

It had taken us ten years to find Jeff. Ten years of careful positioning, of pretending not to know what we knew. Ten years of laying traps we couldn't spring too soon, because the man in the shadows had built himself a fortress of silence and invisibility. It wasn't enough to know who he was. We had to make him move. We had to make him angry.
And Meredith? Meredith had done that for us, beautifully.

The plan was never revenge. It was exposure. And once exposed, Jeff had no real defenses left. Once his identity snapped into the light—once we finally saw his face, knew the body that matched the voice—we did what we were trained to do. What we were always going to do.

I looked at Mark. He nodded. No words were needed.
Then the doorbell rang.
Once. Sharp. Punctual.

Mark moved to stand but paused when I touched his wrist. He understood. Stepped back. I walked to the door alone.

The porch light buzzed faintly overhead as I opened it. She stood exactly where she was supposed to stand—hoodie damp with mist, duffel slung low, eyes hollow but watchful. She couldn't have been more than twenty-two. Skin pale. Nails short. Shoes scuffed. But her spine—her spine was straight.

"You're early," I said, my voice calm, even.
She nodded. Didn't speak.
"That's good," I added. "It means you're still afraid. It means we still have time."
I stepped aside. She entered without hesitation. In the living room, I poured her a glass of water. She didn't ask for anything.

She didn't say her name. I opened the manila folder on the coffee table and showed her the names. Two for surveillance. One for elimination.

She stared at the photos. Her hands didn't shake.
She was ready. Not yet trained, but already chosen.
I saw her—the way I used to see myself. Back before Mark.
I was her once. Not a victim. Not a soldier.
Something in between. Something waiting to decide.
Now?
Now I am something else entirely.
Some women are born to nurture. Others are born to survive.
I was born for precision.
I was born for judgment.

They'll call her brave. They'll call me cruel.
They'll be wrong.
And they'll be right.
The world doesn't need more wives. It needs more
reckoning.

I was never just a good wife.
I was a blade in a silk sheath, waiting for the right hand. And
now?
That hand is mine.

I do it for the forgotten women. The ones who carry it all,
quietly.
The ones who are dismissed, betrayed, used up.
They deserve better.
I'm not here to comfort.
I'm here to eliminate the problem.
Efficiently.
Permanently.
You're welcome.

Epilogue

The hydrangeas had paled to the color of ash, their bloom spent, their beauty quieter now—less showy, more resolved. Claire knelt beside them, gloved hands deep in the soil, her posture relaxed, her expression unreadable.

The camera hidden in the neighbor's roof vent had a clear view, just as it had the day before, and the week before that. She let it see what it came for: the good wife, alone in her garden.

Mark had left hours ago. The car was gone from the driveway, his travel mug rinsed in the sink. A shirt still hung from the closet door, sleeves turned inside out. He was never careless, except for details meant to be noticed.

The girls were inside, loud with morning energy. Their laughter spilled through the kitchen window—real and radiant. Claire took comfort in that. They were still untouched by what their parents had done. By what they *were still doing*.
She stood slowly, brushing soil from her gloves, and looked up—just enough for the lens to catch the shadow in her eyes. To anyone watching, she was tired. Frayed. Alone.
But that was the story they wanted told.

The truth lived in the silence between their glances. The slight tension in Mark's jaw whenever he leaned in for a kiss. The way her fingers had curled twice around the coffee mug that morning—once to hold it, once to signal.

They had never been at odds. Not for a moment. Their marriage was real. Worn, yes. Weathered. But unbroken. Every whispered fight, every slammed door, every brittle silence had been scripted with precision.

For Meredith. For Jeff. For the agency that had once tried to control them. Every movement in their home had been a dance— choreographed and captured, then dissected by enemies who never realized they were watching actors. Experts.

Claire had always been the bait. Mark, the trigger. Now, the roles were blurred.

The surveillance feeds had gone quiet after the final takedown. Jeff was gone. Meredith was buried in the system. There were no more shadows behind the blinds. No more lipstick-stained cups planted on counters. The game was over.

But the work had only just begun.

Now, she was no longer the frightened 22 year old walking down a hotel corridor in uncomfortable heels, she saw herself clearly—not the mother, not the wife, not the woman anyone thought they understood. But the architect. The one who had turned survival into strategy. Grief into weaponry.

Behind her, the house buzzed softly with domestic noise—running water, a cartoon theme song, Emma shouting something to Sadie about strawberries. It grounded her. Gave her purpose. Everything she did now was in service of that quiet. That freedom.

She had women working under her now. Smart, untraceable, fluent in charm and control. They used names like Layla, Brynn, Mara. They walked into rooms built for men who thought money was power, who thought compliance could be purchased. They wore wiretaps and perfume. They carried poison in their purses.

They found the rot.

And Claire? She made sure it never rose again.

She turned from the flowers and stepped into the sunlight, where the world saw only what she allowed.

She was a good wife.

She was a better mother.

And for some men, she was the last face they would ever see.

Acknowledgments

Writing *The Good Wife* was a journey through shadowed hallways and cracked reflections, and I am endlessly grateful to those who walked beside me, both in light and in quiet. To my readers — thank you for opening the door to this world of secrets, survival, and silent strength. Your support makes stories like this possible.

To the women who carry more than they're ever given credit for — this book is for you. For the wives, mothers, sisters, daughters, and friends who keep the world turning while remaining underestimated. Your quiet resilience is the fire beneath every word.

To my inner circle: the trusted few who read early pages, offered honest feedback, and reminded me that the truth is always in the subtext — thank you for your insight, your encouragement, and your ability to see what was never said aloud.

To the storytellers who came before me, and to the ones still clawing through the dark with nothing but a match and a voice — keep going. The world needs your fire.

And finally, to the version of myself who thought she had to be perfect to be worthy — I see you. I'm proud of you. And I'm not writing for perfection anymore. I'm writing for power.

— B.M. Roberts

About the Author

B.M. Roberts has long been captivated by psychological thrillers—the ones that simmer with secrets, unravel domestic facades, and linger long after the final page. Drawn to the hidden fractures beneath seemingly perfect lives, she writes with a sharp eye for emotional nuance, moral tension, and the quiet unraveling of the human psyche.

When she's not writing, she's likely reading something dark and twisty or replaying a conversation in her mind, looking for what wasn't said. She lives in the Midwest with her brilliantly chaotic family and believes the most powerful fiction is the kind that unsettles, provokes—and makes you sleep with the light on.

The Arrangement

Chapter One   Petals for the Dead

The first bloom she touched that morning was already dying.

Violet Vale could tell by the faintest bruise along the petal's edge—a smoky, almost imperceptible undertone of plum feathering through what should have been pure, unmarred ivory. A quiet betrayal. The kind only someone like her would notice. She turned the lily between her fingers with exquisite care, studying it as one might study a confession scrawled in trembling ink—soft, urgent, unwilling to lie. Not hastily. Not sentimentally. But with a reverence reserved for final things.

The shop around her was still cloaked in half-light, the windows opaque with the breath of winter, condensation pooling at their corners like secrets trapped behind glass. The radiator had not yet stirred to life, and the air inside remained hushed and sharp, each breath blooming visibly before vanishing into silence. Outside, the air was stretching its limbs—somewhere in the distance, a car door slammed; a shovel scraped along stone; a dog barked once and fell quiet again. But inside Vale & Bloom, the world remained still, untouched by anything as intrusive as time.

She liked it that way. Needed it.

Opening the shop was a ritual, not a routine.

The blinds remained drawn. The lights stayed dim. The radio—a vintage walnut-cased relic with a rusted dial—sat mute in the corner, its cord unplugged. She had never played music while arranging funerals. It felt wrong, almost obscene. Joy had no business mingling with grief. She preferred the sound of water in the vase, the delicate snip of scissors, the low rasp of stem against stem—those were the holy sounds. Anything more would've felt like trying to entertain the dead.

On the worktable behind the counter, a shallow porcelain basin waited, half-filled with water and the cool green scent of eucalyptus. Next to it, her tools were lined up in perfect order: garden shears, wire snips, silk thread, ribbon the color of ash, a shallow silver bowl holding pearl-headed pins. The air carried a faint perfume—lavender, crushed pine, a trace of something floral and more elusive, like memory warmed by sunlight.
She moved among them silently, a high priestess of sorrow, her motions composed and exacting. No wasted steps. No hesitations. She trimmed the hydrangeas first, angling the blade cleanly

through each stem with a kind of quiet conviction, as though slicing into the soft green tissue of the past itself. Each piece she laid aside without comment, her expression unreadable. Only her hands betrayed her—sure, fluid, intimate in their attention.

It was Elliot Parker's funeral.   Her hands did not tremble.

245

Not when she reached for the sprays of dusty miller, silvery and soft as breath. Not when she selected the exact shade of cream roses that most resembled the curve of his smile.

Not even when she leaned into the basin to cradle a half wilted camellia—its color nearly the same as the sheets they used to share, long ago, when skin and silence were the only currency they exchanged.

She had known, days before the obituary was published, that he had died. Some women feel it—a weight shifting, a coldness behind the ribs, a silence that sharpens like a blade. She had felt it that Thursday morning, alone in the kitchen, when the light caught the edge of her teacup in just the wrong way. She hadn't checked the news. She hadn't needed to.

Elliot Parker had always been predictable, even in death. He'd returned to town three years ago, a little heavier, a little too tan, with a woman half his age clinging to his elbow like expensive perfume. He had found Violet in the back of the church, arranging a memorial spray for someone else entirely. Their eyes had met. He had smiled, crooked and rehearsed.

"Still keeping those strange hours?" he'd asked.

She had smiled back—thin, precise.
He hadn't asked anything more.
Now, the arrangement was nearly complete, and the sun had begun to smear pale gold across the upper panes of glass, lighting the dust motes that drifted lazily through the chill air like pollen from a ruined garden. Violet dipped her hands into a porcelain bowl of cold water laced with bergamot and rosemary, watching the ripples bloom outward from her wrists. She let them soak there a moment longer than

246

necessary, as if cleansing her skin of something intangible—memory, perhaps, or regret.

She dried her fingers slowly on a linen cloth pressed clean with starch, the edges embroidered with her mother's initials—now faded to a dull ghost of thread—and reached for the final bloom.

A black calla lily.

Clean. Sleek. Absolute.

Its stem was glossy and unyielding, its throat dark as ink. She pressed it into the arrangement with care, tucking it slightly off-center where it would draw the eye, but not demand attention. Perfection lived in restraint.

As she anchored it into the mossed foam, her thumb caught the edge of a thorn she'd missed. A thin line opened across her skin, and a single drop of blood surfaced—deep, jewel toned, almost erotic in its suddenness. She held her hand to the light, watching the way it glistened along the delicate ridge of bone.

She did not flinch. She did not wince.

She simply looked.   The
wound was small.   It
would not stain.

She pressed a fresh ribbon to the cut, wrapped it tightly, and moved on.
The bell above the door did not ring so much as it shivered.

Violet looked up.

He entered as though trying not to disturb something sacred, which was almost amusing, considering the weight of arrogance he carried beneath his posture. Men like that always assumed their silence was a kindness. That being quiet was the same as being good. But this one—he paused just inside the threshold, exhaling slowly, scanning the space as if committing every corner to memory.

He was careful. Calculating.
His gaze moved from the door to the floorboards to the counter, then to her. And when it landed—fully, directly—he smiled. Not wide. Not false. Just enough to make a woman feel seen. It was the kind of smile that could be edited to mean anything. Violet didn't return it.

"Sorry," he said, voice soft, low, practiced. "Didn't mean to interrupt."
"You didn't." She gestured to the space around her, bare of customers. "I'm not open yet. But if you're here for something time-sensitive..."

He nodded once, stepping forward into the light.

Close now, she could see he was younger than Elliot had been when they'd met—mid-thirties, maybe. Clean-shaven. Blue eyes, though not the warm kind. No, these were the cold, coin-bright kind. The kind that watched, weighed, recorded. He wore a dark wool coat, expensive but too new, the collar still resisting his neck like a lie not yet settled in.
"I need something for a service," he said. "This afternoon."
A beat. Just long enough.

"For my aunt."

Violet blinked once, slow.

"Condolences," she said politely. Then, "Name of the deceased?"

He hesitated. Only a flicker, but enough.

"Marjorie Smith," he answered. "She was… private. Not many mourners. Just me and a few others."

"Of course," she said, and turned her back to him without further question.

She crossed to a small ledger book at the end of the counter, one she kept not for record keeping but for tone. Color palette, flower temperament, scale. The real orders were digital now, but Violet didn't trust cold things to capture loss properly. She preferred ink. Ink had weight. Ink made mistakes. Ink remembered.

As she uncapped her pen, she could feel his eyes still on her. Not in the clumsy, fidgeting way of those unaccustomed to female grace—but in the focused, absorbing way of someone attempting to study an entire ecosystem without disturbing a single blade of grass.

"You're Violet, right?" he asked.   She didn't look up.

"I am."

"I've heard about your work."

She let the compliment hang. No gratitude offered. No protest either.

"I try to listen," she said instead, her voice like silk pressed through a sieve. "The flowers usually know what they need to say."

When she looked at him again, he was watching her hands, not her face.

She wore no rings.
He looked up, quickly.

"I'm Miles," he said.

"Of course you are."

He blinked. Just once. It almost made her smile.

She turned again, slow and fluid, toward the display wall. From it hung a series of dried arrangements in muted palettes—bone white, shadow gray, oxblood. Not bright. Never cheerful. Her living stems remained chilled in the cooler behind the counter, hidden from view like secrets waiting to be claimed.
She opened the cooler door without invitation, letting the cold spill into the space between them like breath between strangers. The air smelled of violets and green stems and something deeper beneath—earth, perhaps, or loss.

Behind her, Miles spoke.
"I didn't see you at the funeral."

Her hand hovered over a cluster of delphinium.

"I don't attend," she said. "I prepare. There's a difference."

When she turned back, her arms were full of white tulips and blue thistle, small sprigs of myrtle bundled with fine silk cord. She set them gently on the table, arranging them in a way that looked effortless but was not.

"That's beautiful," he said.

She tilted her head, watching him now.
"You haven't seen it yet."

He smiled again. More carefully this time.

Outside, the wind pressed softly against the front windows, rattling the corners of the glass in their antique frames. Violet did not look away.

Miles was lying.

He did not have an aunt. He did not belong to grief. His shoes were too clean. His eyes moved too much. His voice too polished for mourning.

But still, she said nothing.

Not yet.
She began assembling the bouquet without asking his preferences.

The stems spoke more honestly than people did, and Violet had long ago stopped offering choices to the bereaved— especially the ones who weren't really grieving. She chose with precision: a base of white tulips, signifying forgiveness without absolution; blue thistle for

resilience and truth kept sharp-edged; sprigs of myrtle for remembrance, or perhaps possession. The myrtle was always the test.

She didn't rush.
Each element was selected with care and coaxed into place the way a violinist tunes a single string—deliberately, attentively, without apology. The bouquet took shape the way a verdict does: slowly, inevitably.

Across the counter, Miles said nothing. He simply watched her, his gaze steady but never overt. He had the discipline of someone used to being unnoticed. Or someone who had trained himself to vanish while standing in plain sight.

"What did she love?" Violet asked without looking up.

"Who?"

"Your aunt."

She heard the pause before he answered. It came like a missed step on a staircase—almost nothing, but enough to jolt the rhythm of a lie.

"Magnolias," he said. "I think."

Violet turned her head just slightly, the corner of her mouth lifting—not into a smile, but something smaller, sharper. Like the glint of a blade still sheathed.
"We don't use magnolias in mourning," she said quietly. "They rot too fast." He made a low sound in his throat. "I didn't know that."
"No one does." She tied a strip of gray silk around the stems, double-knotted, the ends left long and uneven. "But they're showy. People like the idea of them. It's the scent, mostly. Like clean skin after a long bath."

She said it plainly, and let the words hang in the air between them like perfume.
Miles blinked once, slowly. She didn't have to look up to know he was reassessing her. She could feel it—the subtle change in how he stood, the shifting of his weight, the recalibration. That was the trouble with men who came in pretending to mourn. They thought she was just another quiet woman surrounded by soft things. They thought beauty dulled the blade.

They never remembered that flowers are part of the body too. That death can be arranged. "Are you from the area?" she asked.

He shrugged, casual. "I've been through."

Not an answer.

She offered no reaction, only reached for the cardholder—sleek ivory card stock with a gold border—and slipped it into the ribbon. She didn't hand him a pen.

He didn't ask for one.

"Do you deliver?" he asked.
Her voice was soft. "Only when it matters."   That stopped him. Just for a moment.

He looked at her then—really looked—and Violet allowed it. She stood in the shaft of natural light coming through the front window, back straight, chin slightly lifted, as if she were being painted rather than studied. The sunlight hit the fine, almost imperceptible scar at her hairline and caught on the faint gleam of moisture still clinging to her lower lip. She made no effort to wipe it away.
Something passed between them—brief, unspoken, precise. Miles reached into his coat pocket and pulled out a money clip, counting out bills without looking at them.

"No credit?" he asked.

"No receipts," she answered.

She took the cash without hesitation and turned away to record the total in her ledger. Not under Miles Parker. Not under Marjorie Parker. She wrote a small, perfect number next to a single name:

Arrangement No. 5.

When she looked back up, he was already at the door.

"Thank you," he said, his hand lingering just a beat too long on the handle. Violet inclined her head. "Of course."

He stepped outside, the bell above the door trembling in his wake, and was swallowed by the pale winter light.

She did not watch him go.

Instead, she turned back to the arrangement on the table, now sealed and silent and exact. Her eyes rested on the calla lily at its center—still flawless, still black, still gleaming with the weight of unspoken things.

Violet Vale exhaled, slow and steady.
And then, with hands that had once held love and venom in equal measure, she gently touched the place where the thorn had broken skin.
After he left, the air in the shop didn't settle.

It shifted.
Not outward, not away—but inward, coiling into the crevices between walls and breath and memory, like smoke curling back into a chimney. Violet stood very still in its wake, as if movement might break the spell he had brought in with him.

She didn't need to check the name he gave.

There had been no service scheduled that day for a Marjorie Parker. No calls to confirm an order, no whispers from the usual undertakers, no bulletin in the chapel vestibule. It wasn't that she kept tabs on all the dead—it was that the dead often arrived on schedule. And Violet had always known how to read a calendar that wasn't printed on paper.

He hadn't come for flowers.

He'd come for her.

She moved to the basin at the back of the counter and rinsed her hands again, the water cool and herbal against her skin, this time more ritual than cleanliness. She dried them slowly and watched her own reflection in the glass-fronted cabinet where the rare stems were stored—bleeding hearts, ghost orchids, pale dahlias curled inward like secrets.

She studied herself not for beauty, but for erosion.   Her skin remained flawless, but her expression had thinned over time—grown leaner, more neutral. Her body was still lithe, still lovely in that eerie, classical way that never quite seemed born of this century. But something inside her had hardened. Not into stone. Into glass. Clear. Smooth. Capable of cutting through anything.

Elliot had once said she was the quietest woman he'd ever met—and the loudest thing he'd ever wanted.

He had told her that at night, with his hand on her hip and his breath warm at her ear, like it was a compliment he hadn't meant to give. She hadn't responded. Violet had never been the kind of woman to blush. Praise slid off her skin like water. Desire she could recognize—hunger, too. But adoration? That was what got people killed.

She'd left Elliot, of course. Eventually.

She always left them first, though the order never seemed to matter.

Love was never what did the damage.

It was always the aftermath.

And Elliot—sweet, smug, ambitious Elliot—had always been the kind of man who confused being wanted with being worthy. When she'd ended things, cleanly, without cruelty, he'd stared at her for a full minute before laughing, the sound brittle and ugly.

"You're not even crying," he'd said.

"No," she'd replied softly. "But you are."

He had cried, later. Texts in the middle of the night. Then silence. Then a sighting—he with a newer model in tow, she alone and unbothered. It was the same story, rewritten with different names. A narrative that no longer needed her consent.

Still, she hadn't expected him to die.

And yet, when she saw the notice in the paper—local man found unresponsive in bed, no signs of trauma, suspected aneurysm—she hadn't been surprised. She'd pressed her fingers to the thin sheet of newsprint as if to feel for a pulse beneath the ink. There was none.

That night, she'd left a single white chrysanthemum at the back door of his family's estate. No note. No signature. Just the flower, pure and round and mourning.

She knew they'd know it was from her.

And she knew they wouldn't speak her name aloud.

They never did.

She placed the completed bouquet inside the delivery box with deliberate care, wrapping the stems in damp linen and securing the base with wax paper tied off in jet-black twine. No branded tag. No promotional sticker. Violet didn't advertise grief. If her name was known, it was because the dead insisted on her.

A final spray of mist from her glass atomizer clouded the arrangement in a cool floral hush—bergamot, rosemary, and the faintest trace of cedar, barely perceptible unless you leaned in close. The scent lingered like a memory you couldn't quite place.

When she closed the lid, the room felt smaller.   Contained.

Clean.

It was her only rule: no unfinished business. Not in the shop. Not in her work. The arrangements had to be completed, sealed, witnessed. That was how you kept the dead from coming back. People thought it was grief that haunted a place. But it was neglect. It was what you left unsaid. Unsent. Unburied.

The bell above the door hadn't moved in nearly thirty minutes.

But she still felt him.

Not his presence, precisely, but his residue. Some people had it—the ability to leave something behind without touching anything at all. Miles Parker was one of them. He hadn't come for flowers. He'd come for confirmation. For the shape of her voice, the tilt of her smile, the scent in her air.

She didn't know what he wanted.

But she already knew he would return.

And when he did, he'd ask a better question.

She walked to the back corner of the shop, where the orders were logged in thick, calligraphed ledger pages. Most customers were alphabetical. Some, ceremonial. But a few… a very few… had no surname, no address, no contact number.

She opened to the current page and dipped the nib of her pen in deep violet ink. She wrote with elegant precision, each letter small but exact.

Arrangement No. 5 Client:

Miles ?

Occasion: Pending
Notes: Returned the breath to the room before leaving. Likely to circle back. Dangerous only if rushed.

She closed the ledger and locked it beneath the counter.

Outside, the street had grown paler with the sun's steady rise, the fog thinning into early clarity. Violet crossed the room and adjusted the "Closed" sign on the door, turning it quietly to "Open," though she knew no one would come in for at least another hour.

The town didn't rush its mourning.

And Violet didn't rush her arrangements.

She turned toward the rear of the shop, where the shadows still lived, and let her hand trail across the edge of the countertop as she passed.

Her fingertip brushed something cool.

The ribbon she'd used to bind the earlier bouquet. A single strand had come loose. She lifted it gently, considered its weight, and tucked it into her pocket.

Some things, after all, were worth keeping.

The Arrangement will be available for preorder in November 2025